THE OVERCOAT

Anna Howard

Pen Press

© Anna Howard 2012

All rights reserved

No part of this publication may be reproduced, stored in a retrieval system, or transmitted in any form or by any means, without the prior permission in writing of the publisher, nor be otherwise circulated in any form of binding or cover other than that in which it is published and without a similar condition including this condition being imposed on the subsequent purchaser.

First published in Great Britain by Pen Press

All paper used in the printing of this book has been made from wood grown in managed, sustainable forests.

ISBN 978-1-78003-377-8

Printed and bound in the UK
Pen Press is an imprint of
Indepenpress Publishing Limited
25 Eastern Place
Brighton
BN2 1GJ

A catalogue record of this book is available from the British Library

Cover design by Jacqueline Abromeit

from original sketch by the author

Other books by the author

No Pets For Me
Shop-Girl
Another Free Lunch

This one is for Mandy with her limitless supply of encouragement and hugs.

Foreword

Everyone knows that there are good people, people who are just good, selfless, born that way and never change. Sometimes they are called saints. There are bad people too, deeply and innately bad almost from birth. They are totally selfish with no thought for others. They will cheat, lie, do anything to get their way, even kill. They lack the quality we know of as a conscience and sometimes these people are called sociopaths.

Also everyone knows that there are good things, objects which do not live or breathe. We call them talismans or good luck charms. The forms these take are manifold. Many people keep a lucky pebble with them in a pocket because they found it on a good day or in a special place. A cross, star or amulet worn around the neck is commonplace in all cultures of the world. A pentagram under a doormat will keep bad luck from entering the house, some say. A horseshoe, one of the strongest symbols of good luck, should always be displayed with the sides pointing upwards, never down.

Good things aplenty and it makes one wonder about the opposite, if there could be bad things, inanimate objects which bring nothing but trouble. There are superstitious fears of the number thirteen. If you spill salt, throw some over your right shoulder to drive the gremlin away. But could an object, even a garment shaped to human form, without a brain or life of its own, be so steeped in evil that it might be dangerous to use? And if such objects did exist, what could we call them?

Turn the pages, valued reader. See what you think.

– 1 –

From when he was quite young, Roger Clewes had wondered if there was something the matter with him. It wasn't that he felt unwell or looked sickly. In fact, he was quite handsome in a conventional sort of way, with his dark hair and olive skin tone. He grew up straight and tall, just over six feet and was rather bright at school, particularly at artwork.

When, however, in his teens, all the usual ribaldry and kids' pranks in the toilets began, Roger was made to realise that his penis was minute. That is compared with everyone else present and even his friends insisted on playing comparison games. After that, experiments with erections produced some but not much size improvement.

Later, he was pushed into an experience behind the bicycle sheds with Alice, the school flirt who promised and, indeed, delivered much more. When she got Roger's pants open she was overcome, not by passion but by uncontrollable merriment. It was unfortunate that she failed to keep her glee to herself because poor Roger spent weeks hiding his head under a black cloud of pure mortification.

Mr Carter, his art teacher, was kinder but just as unsuccessful when he found Roger weeping one day in the cloakroom. First he tried talking about it. When this failed to work, he tried a demonstration but all to no avail.

"I think the trouble with you, Clewes, is that you quite simply don't like it," Mr Carter opined sadly. "Stick to your drawing board, forget sex and you'll go far."

He saw the tearstained face looking up at him and felt a genuine compassion and tenderness which also had nothing to do with sex. Being a kind man who would never knowingly harm anyone, he gently patted the boy's head.

"Don't worry," he said. "You're not the only one, you know. Quite a few people feel like that, in fact. I'll still teach you all I know about art and you will be a success, I promise."

He was right, of course. Comforted somewhat by his mentor but still unfulfilled in other directions, Roger decided that sex, whether connected to a female or male partner, was just too much trouble and bother, arousing in him nothing more than mild irritation. However, with a pencil half the thickness of his reluctant organ in his hand, he felt a thrill which pulsed through his body faster than any orgasm.

Best of all, Roger enjoyed drawing clothes, sometimes without people filling them even. He also drew women and men dressed in a kaleidoscope of costume, ranging from evening dresses to swimsuits and even stage clothing. His drawing of the Moor of Venice in full regalia won first prize in a competition and secured him a good job with a High Street fashion house when he left school.

Roger remained with this employer, his salary rising steeply when they discovered that he had a photographic memory. They sent him, first class, to all the top Paris fashion shows. There he would sit throughout, applauding politely each outstanding creation as it drifted past, draped on a skinny, hard-eyed model. Every blink of his eye was the equivalent of a shutter clicking in a forbidden camera.

When he got home, he would spend many happy, exciting hours transferring from his mind's eye to paper the outfits he had seen, each with just one important alteration. Sometimes this would be as small as a button in a different place or as big as a collar added or removed. However, each outfit was changed enough to be a legal original and not a copy, to be sold under the label of his employers. Roger never forgot Mr Carter and his words of comfort and remembered him with warmth and a certain affection.

Everyone assumed Roger was gay, although he was never seen at social events with a man. The only woman he was seen with was his mother, who he adored. She had always hugged him when he was sad, made tasty little meals when was ill and praised him for almost everything he did. Perhaps things might have been different if his father had not died when he was seven. Roger could barely remember him and, even after he had become successful and financially well off, it never occurred to him to move out of the family home and away from the woman he loved.

One Thursday evening, Roger arrived home from a long drawn out irritating business meeting and found his mother in a bit of a state. Usually, she was well into the preparation of whatever delicacies she had planned for dinner by six thirty. On this particular evening, however, she had hardly begun and was hopping around the kitchen, opening and closing the fridge and cupboard doors and muttering to herself. There were no delightful smells to greet Roger, just a harassed sounding "Hello, dear. How was your day?"

"Boring, going over the same old things," replied Roger. "They never seem to grasp that they don't have to tell me about things like the latest quirk in necklines. I need a stiff G and T, How about you?"

"Oh, yes please. I can't seem to get organised. All at sea."

"So what's put you out of sorts? Anything in particular?" enquired Roger, carrying the drinks into the kitchen.

His mother accepted the proffered glass, uncharacteristically taking two greedy gulps before setting it down on the table.

"I went shopping because I fancied another winter coat before the real cold sets in," she explained. "I couldn't find anything I liked and then got harried and pressured by this wretched assistant. She followed me all over the shop on my heels as if I were going to steal the hangers or something. She wouldn't let me look in peace so I gave up and came home but it made me cross and unsettled me a bit."

"Why didn't you tell me you wanted a coat, you silly old love," exclaimed Roger. "I can get you anything you want so easily, you know that."

"Yes I do know, dear, but just for once I thought I'd go off shopping and get something for myself by myself, like other people do," she replied.

"Well, it didn't work, did it? Where is this shop with the wretched assistant?" asked Roger.

"It was the one at the end of the High Street with the curved window going round the corner. It always has something nice in the window, which is why I went in as a last resort," she replied dolefully.

"Very well. Tomorrow morning we are going back there to teach them a thing or two. No arguments," said Roger, holding up his hand when she looked about to say something. "As for now, we haven't had a nice curry for a long time, have we? So I shall go and get us a lamb pasanda takeaway with all the trimmings from that Mr Patel who's in love with you and puts extra meat in."

She blushed and relaxed, looking a lot better, to Roger's relief. He didn't like it if she got upset. It made him feel oddly insecure, as if something awful were about to happen.

"Now you put your feet up and finish your drink," he told her bossily, kissing her on both cheeks.

He took an insulated bag out of the cupboard and departed, waggling his fingers in a little wave.

* * *

– 2 –

In a large expensive house overlooking the river, a man lay slumped in an armchair by a false but realistic looking fire. He was handsome, young looking in spite of the flecks of grey in his hair but his face was drawn with sadness. His right hand, resting on the arm of the chair, held a half full brandy glass. In his left hand was the photograph of a woman. Between sips from the glass, he murmured a kind of mantra, over and over to himself.

"I'm sorry, my darling, so very sorry. I love you so much but it was not enough."

Every so often, he lifted the photograph to his lips and kissed it, leaving little smears of moisture on the glossy surface. Presently he rose and made his way a little unsteadily to a glazed cabinet and fumbled inside until he found another bottle of brandy. He returned to his chair and after refilling his glass, he propped the photograph against the bottle and took a cigar from the box on the table, still mumbling to himself.

"I promised you. I made you a coat which was the best, the finest thing I have ever done in my life, my whole life. For my darling wife that you should get better and wear it for me."

It took the man three attempts to light the cigar and two more to refill his glass before he picked up the photograph again. He peered into the face of the woman, dropping cigar ash down the front of his shirt as he attempted to kiss her once more.

"I promised you would be the only one ever to wear this masterpiece of a garment. If only you could live. But I broke my promise."

The tears came then and fell to join the cigar ash, making grey streaks on his white shirt. He cried silently, with a kind of dull despair, his face mirroring what was in his heart. After a while, he grew calmer and noticed the mess he had made. He even managed a weak giggle.

"Mucky bugger," he said, trying to brush his front and hold the glass in the same hand, splashing brandy everywhere.

He put the glass down and picked up his cigar, wagging it at the photograph. He knew he would have a gummy mouth and a headache the next day.

"You're going to be cross with me for this," he slurred, "but I can't help it. You died, my darling, and I broke my promise. I let that awful Lehman woman, who never leaves me alone, have your lovely coat. Just to get rid of her. To make her stop. I will never sell it, I told her. It belongs to my darling wife forever, I said. But she just went on and on at me. I should never have left it in the showroom but they wouldn't let me leave it beside your bed."

The man took another huge gulp from his glass and the tears came again. He kissed the photograph between hiccupping sobs until he became calmer and picked up his cigar once more, which was still only half smoked. The house was quiet. His eyelids began to droop and his breathing became regular. The hand holding his cigar relaxed on the arm of the chair and a long blob of ash fell off the end.

Slowly, the cushion began to smoulder. Tiny spirals of smoke drifted upwards towards the sleeping man. He dreamed of his wife on their honeymoon many years before, her laughter and the touch of her hands caressing him. Gently, inexorably, the smoke entered his body.

The heat of the cigar met the warm, split brandy, causing an explosion of flame. The man slept on, safe in the past with his love.

– 3 –

It was Friday and the end of the working week was nearly there. Elsie Lehman was looking forward to a pleasant lunch date with a few friends. They were meeting at a newly opened bistro in the High Street to test the social and culinary worth. Elsie felt no really deep affection for these friends but liked to be seen about town. After all, she was a member of the Chamber of Commerce, which stood for something in a fashionable small town like Minchester.

Her husband, David, had been a successful businessman and had always lavished gifts upon her as well as love. She returned that love with attention and fidelity but they never had children. He was, as some envious people hastened to point out, more than old enough to be her father and perhaps too old to be a father himself. Elsie always turned a deaf ear to such suggestions and continued to love, honour and obey. In her opinion, this promise included looking attractive, well dressed, being sexy only when appropriate, learning Cordon Bleu cookery and agreeing with all her husband's ideas.

When David died, after suffering three strokes each more massive than the one before, Elsie found herself a fairly wealthy woman in her own right. This fact failed to lessen the genuine grief that she felt but made it more comfortable to bear. A year of mourning passed before she woke up to the fact that she was entirely alone and could now do whatever she pleased without concerning herself with the wishes of others.

Elsie's immediate reaction was to pick out a new horror book from the shelf by her bed and go off to the Sea Dragon Chinese restaurant where they had a sumptuous evening buffet laid out to help oneself. David always abominated

Chinese cuisine. She sat in solitary state at a table for two, reading her book and rising every so often to replenish her plate from the vast array of exotic delicacies.

Later in bed that evening, full of Kung Po chicken and king prawns, she lay back contentedly to examine her inner thoughts.

For many years, she had cradled a secret dream. This was to own a small fashion boutique; choosing all original clothes herself from the lesser designers and not too expensive. Next day, after a good night's dreamless sleep and spurred on by her restaurant adventure, she went out and began to patrol the High Street to look for a suitable shop property. Within weeks, she found the one she wanted on a prominent corner and signed a ten-year lease. A month later, the shop was fitted out, decorated, furnished and all but ready to open, all but the name.

Elsie agonised over the name. It needed to be personal yet unique and different. Lehman seemed too hard and Elsie impossible, out of the question. Then she remembered receiving a letter from her opticians once and they had spelled her named incorrectly. Getting the letters in the wrong order, they called her Mrs Elise Lehman. Elise looked and sounded just right, perfect for a shop in Minchester High Street.

The very next day the name was registered, the signwriter got on with the board above the windows and the printer got on with the cards and receipt books. Elise was born and Elsie set off happily with her shopping list to find suitable stock, new cheque book snug in her handbag.

She trawled through the designer establishments that she favoured for her personal requirements, choosing skirts, suits, day and evening dresses and coats. Hats and shoes she decided to leave alone in courtesy to another boutique at the other end of the High Street. Invitations were issued to an equally carefully chosen number of friends and business people to attend an afternoon opening with early cocktails to follow.

It was an overwhelming success. Thousands of pounds had been paid into the new banking account at the end of that opening week and Elsie's accountant warned to sharpen his attention. When Elsie did something, she studied form and did it properly. She remained successful and her attachment to her shop and all it stood for grew consistently from then on.

This particular and fateful Friday, however, was a departure from the usual routine that had evolved over the years. Elsie always opened the shop at half past nine, then left her current assistant in charge, returning before five to see to the daily takings and lock up. On this day, the assistant had asked to go to the dentist, so Elsie had to mind the shop until noon and then go on to her luncheon appointment. She let the assistant think she was doing her a great favour but in fact, she was looking forward to looking after her beloved shop by herself for a few hours.

Good assistants were not easy to find and this one, named Becky, did not yet merit any favour in Elsie's opinion. For instance, she continually forgot to apply the rules and technique of shopkeeping that Elsie tried to teach her, claiming that they were difficult and 'sort of unfair'. One such rule was that the Customer is Always Right. Elsie insisted that this applied, whatever the customer said, asked for or did, provided it was legal, of course. Becky said that the customer was sometimes extremely rude and that she was not going to take that, not from anybody.

Another rule was Leave the Customer to Choose in Peace. Becky argued that she would hardly ever sell anything that way, as most customers really had no idea what they wanted. In spite of all this, the girl was honest and could be trusted to treat the clothes with the respect they deserved. Nevertheless, Elsie enjoyed making her grovel a little for some time off.

This morning, Elsie examined her reflection in her long mirror with pleasure. Her figure was still trim and the peachy tones in the suit she chose to wear complemented

closets at the side. A chaise longue in an elegant Art Deco style and covered with pink brocade stood halfway down the showroom in front of a drooping ficus shrub. At the far end, somebody was seated at a desk.

"Go and sit down, dear," Roger whispered, indicating the couch to his mother, then went briefly to examine two rails of coats.

He returned quickly to Marian when he realised that she was having difficulty and took her arm to raise her to her feet again. The woman sitting at the desk got up and approached them.

"Good morning," said Elsie cheerfully. "Is there something I can do for you?"

"Yes," replied Roger briskly. "Kindly bring a chair for my mother. This sofa is much too low for her."

Somewhat taken aback, Elsie could only think of the chair behind her desk and went to fetch it.

"Roger, that isn't..." Marian began to say, plucking at her son's sleeve.

"Hush, darling. Leave everything to me," whispered Roger.

Elsie was wondering who this rather insignificant looking elderly lady could be. Certain that she had never seen her or the man before, she was surprised to be spoken to in this manner. She returned with the chair and stood by whilst the man settled his mother into it, having removed her rather ordinary camel hair coat and laid it on the chaise, first brushing some invisible specks of dust from the pink brocade. For some reason, this gesture annoyed Elsie intensely. She waited, saying nothing.

"Now," said Roger, turning to face Elsie, "we are here to choose an overcoat for the winter. If you have something that is suitable, of course," he added, as if an afterthought or a distinct negative possibility.

This irritated Elsie even more. She had to remind herself of her own rules, such as The Customer is Always Right and Never Show Impatience.

the remains of the summer tan still left tinting her skin. As she attached the amber earrings which were David's last present to her, she wondered if she could afford a week in Majorca later on to top the tan up a little. It was not the financial cost that worried her but leaving the shop for a whole week.

She took her new coat, as yet unworn, from its hanger and held it against her body. The picture in the mirror became even more pleasing to her. It was a unique model, a one-off which was acquired only two days before and after a great deal of persuasion on her part. Gently, she caressed the coat and smoothed the collar, smiling at her reflection. It had cost her six hundred pounds and worth every penny, because she knew she would be the envy of her lunch companions later.

"Dear Anton," she murmured to herself. "I can usually wheedle you into giving me what I want."

Outside the sun shone and it was warm for October, almost as if summer were reluctant to leave. Elsie almost took her new coat back indoors, as she stood on the step and revelled in the illusion. Then she remembered the role she wanted it to play and decided to carry it on her arm. It was only a short walk from the flat to the shop.

Elsie dawdled a little, enjoying the warmth and the tubs of colourful chrysanthemums supplied by the council at the side of the road. It was a few minutes past opening time when she unlocked the shop door and entered her special kingdom, pressing the code numbers on the alarm as she passed.

All was in order, as she had left it the night before. With a little frisson of happiness, Elsie went slowly past the rows of clothing to the desk right at the back. She turned on the spotlights and hung her coat up carefully on a hanger. Then she sat down, took the pens and receipt books out of the drawer and settled down to wait for the trading day to begin.

* * *

– 4 –

Someone else on that Friday morning was en flowers and sunshine in the High Street. Marian on the bench outside the bank for a short while the world go by and waiting for her son. Roger a to the bank on a Friday morning to get what h 'weekend indulgence cash'. What he spent it on idea and never asked. He earned it and, as far concerned, he should do whatever he liked with

Eventually Roger reappeared. He was dres in pale fawn corduroys, an open-necked shirt jacket with leather patches on the elbows. (with a smile, his mother thought he looked v: gentleman farmer or an off duty police inspecto

"Come along, dear. Upsy daisy. We have task to perform," he said, helping her to her fee

They walked to the end of the High Stree on the corner, outside the shop. One window v a long dress of a silky material in deep lilac window, the model was rather cleverly ar down in a high-backed wicker chair and wea coloured pleated skirt which fell open to glimpse of thigh. The white blouse on top h the first one undone to emphasise a hint of cle

"I do like that," Marian murmured dreami such interesting and attractive windows in thi

"Not for you, that one. Far too young a said Roger. "In we go."

He opened the door, which gave a discree and shepherded his mother inside. She stood a few moments while he looked around. H there were probably twenty-five coats h

"Does Madam have any specific style or colour in mind?" she asked in as mild a tone as she could muster and fixing a smile in place.

"My *mother*," said Roger firmly, "is a size fourteen and does not like black. Our taste in style is impeccable and any other colour would be considered. That should give you plenty of scope."

Elsie just stood there, dumbfounded, wondering what gave this man the authority to speak to her, or at her would be a better description, in such a way in her own shop. He certainly looked as ordinary as any other man and not wealthy either in his cords and patched jacket.

"The best thing would be," Roger went on, suddenly favouring Elsie with a cold gaze, "for you to bring an example in size fourteen, one at a time, of whatsoever stock in coats that you may have for our consideration. Remembering, of course, not to include anything black."

He turned away and it took Elsie a long moment to pull herself together. She moved to the rails of clothes with a murmured "Certainly, Sir," uttered purely out of habit and in slightly shocked bewilderment.

"Roger, I must tell you—" said Marian, frantically tugging at his arm.

"Now you must hush," he interrupted. "Trust me. Just sit there, look at the coats and enjoy the trip."

Elsie selected a coat in the correct size, which was also her own size and therefore always commanded special attention when she was buying. This one had come from a small but talented designer from the neighbouring county. She took it and laid it reverently on the chaise in an attitude of display and stood back.

"Thank you. You may wait," said Roger.

Elsie seethed and took another step backwards. Roger lifted the coat, smiled at his mother and said, "Upsy daisy, dear."

Obediently, Marian stood up, held out her arms and the coat slipped on. It fitted perfectly and she did a little twirl.

She and Roger had a brief discussion which Elsie was unable to quite catch, something about sleeves. Then the coat was removed and handed back to her.

"You may bring the next one," said Roger.

Now in an odd kind of trance, Elsie took the coat and the same performance was repeated with another one. Again it was rejected until, after six more tries, Elsie ran out of examples in size fourteen. Except for black ones. She stated this fact, finding a new crispness in her voice, bordering on pleasure.

Elsie had decided that these people had no intention whatever of buying a coat but were just having a game. Well, that could be played by both sides. The alternative was, of course, that someone who knew her fixed principles was testing her. Possibly one of her fellow members of the Chamber of Commerce. That could be made to backlash too, thought Elsie and smiled gently to herself.

"I'm sorry I am unable to fill your needs," she said, in what she hoped was a sufficiently humble voice.

"Oh, we haven't finished yet," snapped Roger with a frosty glare in her direction.

He moved towards the display rails, leaving Elsie furious once more. Suddenly, he turned on his heel.

"What," he demanded, "is that coat hanging there at the very back? Is *that* one a size fourteen?"

"As a matter of fact it is," replied Elsie, "but—"

"And it is *not* black, is it?" said Roger.

"No, but—"

"Then bring it," instructed Roger, slowly and kindly, as if speaking to a simpleton.

Elsie could barely contain her rage. Swiftly she strode to the back of the shop, took her coat from its hanger, brought it back and handed it to Roger without a word. In equal silence he took it, held it out for his mother and she slipped her arms into it.

The rich, deep green of the coat seemed to shimmer in a shaft of sunlight as Marian drew its folds around her. One large long button made of some kind of polished bone or wood held the sides together and a collar of soft velvet came around to cradle the neck like a shawl wrapping a baby. The velvet was repeated in deep, roomy cuffs at the ends of the sleeves.

"Turn around, dear. Give us a lovely twirl," said Roger thoughtfully, watching his mother as she caressed the collar.

When he had first spotted the coat, he thought he recognised something and now he knew. As she spun round, the skirt swung out almost in a complete circle, showing a glimpse of silken liner.

"You really like it, don't you, Mother?" he asked.

"Oh, yes. Yes, dear, I do," she replied softly.

"Then it's yours," he said decisively. "My gift to my best friend and dearest Mama. So take it off now, dear."

Elsie was listening and watching with the feeling of being in a nightmare, unable to wake up. This was *her* coat they were talking about. Her mind began to work at top speed, suddenly.

"I can find no price ticket on this coat," announced Roger. "How much is it?"

"It's a very special coat, which is why there is no ticket," said Elsie with a little smirk. "The price of this coat, the only one of its kind, is nine hundred pounds."

She was sure the joke was over now. If this was a test, it had gone far enough. Even if these two were, by some chance, cocky but real customers, it was far too much money for them. So certain was Elsie, that she turned away and picked up her coat to return it to its hanger.

"We would like it packed to take with us please, not to be delivered," came the now hated voice from behind her and she almost dropped the coat on the floor in her astonishment.

"We cannot accept credit cards and even with a guarantee, a cheque will take four days to clear, so you will be unable to take the coat today," said Elsie, recovering quickly.

"This will be a cash transaction. Please ensure that the packing is adequate," came the dry voice yet again.

Elsie saw to her horror that a series of fifty pound notes were being counted out on to the low table by the chaise. She was left with one hope; that the notes were actually forgeries. Quickly, she gathered them up with the coat and took them to test in the X-ray machine on her desk.

The money was, of course, genuine. There was nothing more Elsie could do. She packed her coat in tissue paper, placed it in one of her largest pink and gold carriers and gave it to Roger. He took it, said 'Good Morning' with a curt nod and he and his mother left.

Blindly, Elsie went to the back of the shop and into the small toilet. Here, she did something she had not done for a long time, since her husband had died in fact. She sat down, put her arms on the wash basin, laid her head on them and cried.

*

Roger and Marian walked home with their purchase, past the flowers in the warm sunshine.

"Thank you so much, dear," Marian said to her son. "I do really love that coat but you know, that wasn't the person I saw in that shop yesterday. She was a youngster and this was a much older woman today. That's what I kept trying to tell you but you wouldn't let me."

Roger stopped and looked at her, then burst out laughing.

"That silly, vain woman was probably the owner then," he said when he had regained his breath.

"Oh, heavens! You did give her a very hard time, you know."

"Don't worry about it," said Roger, still chuckling. "She deserved all of that for not training her assistant properly. And I'm sure that coat is something very special. We'll see in a minute."

When they got home, he unwrapped the coat and began to examine it in detail from top to bottom. Slightly mystified by the faint aroma of Arpège perfume, he wondered if the woman was silly enough to spray the shop and then charge more.

Then in the lining, near the right arm, he found a tiny label with a name embroidered in white silk. The name was Anton Paloma.

"There!" he exclaimed. "I knew it! Look, Mother. This is Tony Pidgen, one of my tutors at art college. He became one of the top designers and his work is sought everywhere. This coat is one of his and an absolute bargain."

"I'm glad of that, darling," said Marian, a touch dryly, "because I did think it was rather a lot of money."

"You're worth it, best mother in the world," replied Roger. "Now go and hang your lovely new coat up because it's too warm for it today. Then we'll go and have lunch at that little place by the river."

Patting his cheek, she smiled and did as she was told.

* * *

– 5 –

Marian was happy. She was happy because in a few hours her son would be home again. He had telephoned the previous evening from Rome, where he was staying to cover two big fashion shows. It was four rings before she answered because it was in the middle of *EastEnders* on the television and she had to turn the sound down. She was not expecting the call and was overjoyed to hear his terse "Hello, Ma. It's me."

"Roger darling, how nice. Are things going well in Rome?"

"Yes. In fact I'll be finished early tomorrow. I'll get the lunchtime plane back and be home for dinner."

"Oh, good. Have you been eating well and sleeping?"

"Yes fairly. But please, no pasta for a few days. OK?"

"Of course, dear, and I'll be sure to get up bright and early."

"Huh? What for?" asked a slightly mystified Roger, who was tired.

"Well, there are menus to plan and I may have to go to the shops and—"

"No, no. Not tomorrow," interrupted Roger, suddenly rather exasperated with being mothered so thoroughly, even over the telephone. "I've just decided. We'll be going out for dinner to that new French place in the High Street. Would you ring them and book a table for 7.30?"

"Very well, dear. I'll look forward to it. Have a safe journey and I'll see you tomorrow."

Nevertheless, Marian did get up early and decided to bake a batch of her son's favourite cakes and biscuits. Now the house was redolent with warm, homely smells of brownies and walnut slices. Cooking and baking were the main ways in which she could show her love for him.

Putting her efforts to cool on the big dresser top, she idly wondered, not for the first time, why Roger had never married. As far as she knew, he had never even had a steady girlfriend or if he had, he must have kept it a secret. With no father or other male family member left to influence their lives, Marian worried in the early years about whether, by herself, she was doing all the right things bringing up her son.

The only other female Roger ever showed affection or interest was his much younger cousin, Nancy. From the age of two, she would ride on the tall, gangling Roger's shoulders, shouting "Giddy up" and holding on to his hair. He was always patient with her, even when she kicked him in the chest with her little bare feet in an effort to make him run faster. As she grew, he would take her to the park and push her on the swings, never tiring at the continuous appeals of "More, more, Roggie."

In her teens, he advised Nancy on dress and hairstyles. In fact he was the only person the by then headstrong girl would even listen to. It was always Roger she ran to after failed first dates with gauche and clumsy beaus. When she elected to remain in England to study at the age of 22 when her parents went to live in Australia, it was Roger who lulled their fears by vowing to guard and protect her.

As they always seemed so close, Marian dared to hope that the relationship might develop into something more, in spite of the age difference. After all, even if Nancy was the only daughter of her sister and therefore Roger's first cousin, there was nothing at all harmful in the family to be inherited and enhanced by marriage. But it was not to be. Roger remained just her champion and special confidant and she met and fell in love with a young, newly qualified doctor. Roger's approval was sought, as it was with almost everything and he finally helped to find them a flat when they wanted to set up home together.

The couple seemed very happy, although Roger saw slightly less of Nancy than before. She qualified as a beautician and Roger's gift to her was a celebration dinner at one of his favourite restaurants. It was a family affair, just the four of them and a great success. The aptly named Luke and Roger had obviously formed some kind of bond and got on well. Luke was another only child and Marian could sense an older brother element creeping into the relationship and she was glad.

Looking at her array of the morning's baking still cooling off, Marian was reminded that it had been several weeks since they had seen Nancy and Luke. She thought it might be a good idea to invite them round to tea soon to catch up with news. Then her mind turned to Roger coming home and going out to dinner. This new restaurant had good reports in the local paper but they had not yet tried it.

Suddenly, she remembered her coat, the one that Roger bought for her. She had not yet worn it and there was a definite seasonal chill in the late November air. How appropriate it would be, she thought, to wear Roger's gift for the first time to be taken to dinner at a new restaurant for the first time. She chuckled to herself. With his sense of curtain up occasion, Roger would appreciate that.

She made herself a milky coffee and a sardine sandwich for lunch, her favourite but hated by Roger, and took it into the sitting room to watch the television while she ate. This was also a habit which Roger abhorred but she found it relaxing, particularly after a morning standing in the kitchen beating hell out of cake ingredients in a bowl.

*

Marian woke with a start to the sound of the blonde girl reading the weather forecast and looked at her watch.

"Oh my heavens, it's a quarter to three and I haven't even rung the restaurant," she muttered crossly to herself.

"There is a severe frost warning for the south, so take care," said the blonde weather girl.

"Oh, shut up," replied Marian, switching her off and reaching for the telephone.

A man with a charming French accent took the booking for a table for two and called her chère Madame, which made her feel a little better. She washed up her sandwich plate so that there would be no trace of sardine and went upstairs to shake out the folds of her new coat and decide what to wear with it. Then a nice long, hot bath with lots of lily-of-the-valley oil would be just the thing, she thought. She began to feel a frisson of expectation and excitement, like someone going on a date.

Just as Marian reached the top of the stairs, the doorbell rang. She stopped, wondering who it could be at this time of day. It could be someone selling something, of course, or maybe not.

"Oh, I'd better go and see," she sighed, feeling cross again now that her mood was shattered.

She turned sharply, caught her foot in the bannister railing of the top step and plunged headlong down the stairs to the hall at the bottom.

The woman on the doorstep thought she heard a faint sound from within the house. When nobody came, she rang the bell again and waited but there was nothing. After a while, looking reluctantly over her shoulder, she went away.

* * *

– 6 –

Luke came out of the station at a fast trot. He was looking for the little blue car, whose driver had not been waiting on the platform to greet him as usual. There it was, in the corner of the car park with Nancy still sitting behind the wheel. She got out and ran to him as soon as she saw him, hugging him with unusual intensity.

"I'm so glad you're back," she mumbled, pressing her body tightly against his and pushing her face into his neck.

"Wow! I'll go away more often if it has this effect," said Luke, wrapping arms around her. "I'm sure I can find another seminar somewhere next week."

"Don't you dare," she retorted, going round to the passenger side of the car and climbing in. "Home, Benson," she added, when Luke got in beside her and turned on the ignition.

*

"The silence around here is deafening," he commented five minutes later, after overtaking a petrol tanker and neatly avoiding a young lady who pushed a pram which possibly held her most precious possession off the kerb and into his path. "Are you really so cross with me or is it something else?"

"No, I'm not cross with you, my love. Just thinking."

"Oh, dear. What about?" he asked cautiously.

They had been together for nearly three years and in that time Luke reckoned that he had got to know his Nancy fairly well. This might well be a serious thinking bout because she was not normally quiet for so long. Not unless she was listening to someone else, that is. Perhaps she had done something impulsive which had turned out badly, he thought, like the time she had tried to mend their cuckoo clock. He could never fathom how she managed it but instead of popping its head out and shouting 'Cook-OO', the poor creature fell out like a drunk tripping over a doorstep and moaned 'ooo-ooo-oh' dismally before dragging itself back inside.

Or it could be the thing that Luke secretly feared the most, that she had met somebody else. Somebody a bit better than an ordinary looking doctor whose special interest was Down's Syndrome and who would possibly end up just a country GP for the rest of his life.

"I'll tell you when we get home and I've got a glass of wine in my hand," said Nancy.

Luke shuddered imperceptibly, convinced that if she needed a bit of Dutch courage, the news of her thoughts must come into the second category and wondered who the lucky fellow could be. As a general rule, Luke was a mentally stable and intelligent sort of chap, as a doctor ideally should be. But Nancy was his Achilles heel.

They drew up outside the tiny mews property which Luke had bought to be near the hospital. Without a word, Nancy made for the kitchen. Luke dumped his overnight bag in the hall and followed her. He opened the fridge, found a bottle of Gewurztraminer and a jar of olives which he put down on the table. He pulled the cork with that satisfying sound and solemnly filled the two glasses which Nancy produced from the cupboard. Then he opened the jar of olives, which were his weakness, then drew out a chair and sat.

"Now," he said sternly, "deliver, woman. Or earn my displeasure."

His heart sank as, without even a shade of her usual grin, Nancy picked up her glass and leaned back, resting her bottom on the edge of the sink. She took a long sip, her eyes seeking his over the rim of the glass.

Oh, dear God. Here it comes, Luke thought to himself.

"It's Aunt Marian," said Nancy in a trembly, almost fearful voice. "She's dead."

"What?" said Luke, after staring at her for a moment. "When? Why?"

"Yesterday. They rang me. The police. They were there and Roger was…"

Her glass clattered on the draining board as she shakily tried to put it down. Blindly she stretched her hands out to him.

"It was awful. So awful," she stammered.

Luke was up, round the table in seconds with his arms around her and she fell against him.

"All right. It's all right. I'm here. Now calm down and tell me from the beginning."

Slowly the shaking stopped and Nancy reached for her glass and took a few swallows of wine.

"A policewoman rang from the house. She said there had been an accident and could I come to help my cousin. Roger was in a terrible state when I got there. I couldn't see Aunt Marian but there was an ambulance and I supposed she was in it. There were police everywhere. Roger was hysterical and kept telling them to hurry."

"What time was this?" asked Luke.

"About tea time, four thirty or five. Roger had been away, in Rome I think and had not long been home. His bag was in the hall. He saw me then and begged me to stay and look after the house because he had to go in the ambulance with Aunt Marian. He went off then and I stayed with the policewoman and a policeman who was writing notes."

She paused and took another gulp of her wine while Luke watched her thoughtfully.

"Go on, darling. What happened next?" he asked.

"Well, I asked what was going on and they said they had responded to a call from Roger. They arrived to find the front door open and Roger sitting at the bottom of the stairs holding Aunt Marian in his lap. He said he found her there when he came home and she'd hurt her head and he didn't know what to do, so he dialled 999. She'd obviously fallen because one of her shoes was at the top of the stairs and the other on her foot. They said her neck was broken and she was dead but Roger didn't seem to believe them."

The shaking had stopped and Nancy snuggled closer against Luke, taking the odd sip of wine between sentences. He kept quiet and let her go at her own pace.

"They were very kind. They said they had to stay and make enquiries because it was an accidental death, so I made some tea. After a while, a police car brought Roger home and I said I would stay with him. He was quieter and drank some tea, then took his bag upstairs. But he kept saying it was his fault for not getting home earlier and that he had tried to put her head straight because it was the wrong way round but he couldn't manage it. Oh, poor, poor Roger."

Then Nancy started to cry, burying her head in Luke's neck and letting the sobs come. He held her, rocking gently as if she were a baby.

"I stayed and tried to get him to eat something," she went on when the storm of tears had passed, "but all he would have was tea and a brownie. I think Aunt Marian must have been baking because there were cakes all over the kitchen on cooling racks. I helped him put them away in tins and then he said he was going to bed. I rang this morning and he said everything was OK, but he wasn't going to work because there were a lot of arrangements to attend to. But he sounded a bit weird, you know. I do love him. I know he's rather stuffy but I've always loved my cousin Roger and he's always been there for me."

"Yes I know, love. I'll tell you what we'll do. We'll go round there now and see how things are. Have you still got a spare key to the house?"

"Mm, although I've never used it," Nancy nodded. "It was just supposed to be for dire emergencies only."

"This may well be one of those so take it with you just in case. I'll go and get into my knight's uniform. I think the white charger was put out to grass, so we'll have to take the car instead. Better take my apothecary bag as well."

Luke noticed gratefully that he had managed to raise a watery smile on Nancy's anxious face. He hated it when she got upset. It made him feel so utterly helpless.

It was only a ten minute drive to the other side of town, even through the approaching rush hour. There were no lights showing in the house and Luke fancied that the bell had a hollow ring. He and Nancy looked at each other and Nancy lifted her shoulders in a tiny shrug. Then they heard a shuffling sound and something being dropped on the floor.

The door opened suddenly and Roger was there, gazing at them a little vacantly and looking rather less than his usual dapper self. He was wearing a loose-fitting jumper and his hair had a rumpled-every-five-minutes look.

"Hello. Sorry, I was upstairs tidying things. Come in," he said in an odd staccato voice, like an amateur actor reading a script.

"Oh, Roger," exclaimed Nancy and flung her arms round him, pushing him back from the door.

He rested his chin on the top of her head and absentmindedly stroked her hair. Luke closed the front door and threw an arm across Roger's shoulders. If anyone were watching, they would have seen a picture of compassion and family solidarity. For a brief moment, the three of them stayed like that, motionless and quietly arrested in time.

"We're here, Roger," said Luke, breaking the silence. "We came as soon as I got back from the frozen north, Chester to be more accurate."

"Thank you. I was just going to make some coffee to go with what appears to be the entire contents of a high class patisserie. Do you mind the kitchen? Maybe you know why mother was doing so much baking."

Roger staggered very slightly as he turned into the kitchen doorway and seemed to be disorientated. Nancy wanted to keep hold of him, as if the warmth of her body could put things right.

"I don't suppose you got much sleep last night," commented Luke, regarding him with his shrewd doctor's eye.

"Oh, no. There was far too much to do. There has to be an inquest, you know, because it was an accident. I can't have a funeral until after the inquest. That's the law, I think. But there's still so much to do."

This rambling in an other worldly sort of voice confirmed to Luke that Roger was suffering from shock. Eating something sweet was not such a bad idea in the circumstances.

"Could you make that tea instead of coffee, Roger?" he asked. "And I for one could do with a nice cake or two. Haven't eaten since breakfast."

Thinking of Pinocchio, he touched his nose as he glanced at Nancy for support as was glad to see a smile in her eyes.

"Yes. Me too, Roger," she said. "Are there any nutty ones?"

With a little shake of his head, like someone waking from a doze, Roger said, "Of course. Please sit down. The kettle's on the boil and it won't take a moment. I'm so glad you're here."

They sat. They chatted. Roger encouraged them to eat cakes and Luke encouraged Roger to drink two cups of tea laced heavily with sugar. The whole scene had a vaguely surrealist feel about it. Finally Luke went out to the car and came back with his bag. After a short fumble inside, he produced two small tablets.

"Now, Roger," he said. "I want you to take these with some more tea and possibly another of those delicious cakes." Obediently, Roger poured more brew into his cup, swallowed the tablets down and selected a small chocolate truffle.

"You'll have a good night's sleep now and we'll see you tomorrow," Luke said. "Anything you need before then, phone. OK?"

*

Looking back as they got into the car, Nancy and Luke saw the downstairs light go out and the one upstairs go on.

"He'll be all right for now," said Luke. "Don't worry, love.

"Do you realise it'll be Christmas in three weeks?" said Nancy.

"I know. It creeps up on you doesn't it? The dust will have settled by then and Roger can come to us. I know I sound a bit hard but somebody's got to be practical in the middle of grief."

"Yes, true," responded Nancy. "What about your father?"

"He can come, too. They get along fairly well together. We can all have a different sort of Christmas, mucking about in the mews. Any more problems?"

"Well, there is one thing," replied Nancy. "I went round there yesterday after lunch because we haven't seen them for quite a while. Aunt Marian wasn't there. There was no answer, although I rang the bell twice. You don't think…"

"No, I don't, so stop right there. She'd probably just popped out to get more ingredients for her baking session. You playing merry hell on the doorbell had absolutely nothing to do with her falling downstairs, OK?" said Luke decisively and started up the car.

"I do love you," said Nancy gratefully, leaning over and kissing him on the ear, making him wriggle.

"It may sound quite disgusting after all that cake," said Luke, "but do you know what I fancy? A nice big helping of greasy cod and chips from the local."

"Yuk. Unless eaten with fingers from the paper and washed down with a few glasses of that Australian Riesling you've got in the fridge."

"You betcha," said Luke, grinning with relief that she was no longer so upset and he turned off towards Harry's Hakery.

* * *

– 7 –

Along the High Street, the daffodils in tubs were past their best and had taken on that slightly dusty look of a paler yellow. March was drawing to a close. As a last act of defiance, a keen wind whistled round corners, making the men hunch into the collars of their jackets like tortoises and women hurry past shops without even glancing at the windows.

Three streets away in Roger's house, Nancy was sitting at the top of the stairs, lost in thought and wondering what to do next. She decided not to do anything else until Luke arrived just in case it had to be done all over again and bumped down the stairs on her bottom like she had done as a child. Ignoring the boxes in the hall, she went to the kitchen and put the kettle on.

*

Christmas had been pretty good, considering. Even a little surprising in some ways. On Christmas Eve it had snowed quite hard, covering tubs and window sills in the mews and giving the whole place an almost Dickensian look. Nancy had finished decorating a little tree and was busy stuffing the goose when Gerald, Luke's father arrived, puffing and blowing, arms laden with parcels and bags. He lived thirty miles away and was going to stay, sleeping on the voluminous sofa which turned into a bed. That evening the three of them spent gossiping and catching up over a Chinese takeaway with plenty of wine.

Roger arrived next morning after first ringing up to make sure everything was 'still on'.

"You betcha," was Luke's sound reply, "but you'd better get a move on because we can't and won't start without you. See you in a minute."

*

They had a splendid lunch. The goose was tender, moist and succulent and they had carrots and leeks with it because everybody hated sprouts. The pudding flamed and the mince pies had just the right amount of spice. Afterwards they opened all the enticing parcels under the tree, oohing and ahing appropriately between sips of brandy. It was difficult finding a present for Roger in the circumstances but Nancy finally decided on a sort of I.O.U. for a hairstyle and cut, with an expensive face massage in the gentleman's section of the salon that she worked with.

They spent the rest of the day after the Queen's speech in games of bagatelle on an antique board complete with its original balls, a present from Gerald. There was a lot of shouting, giggling and, towards the end, cheating. For the first time since his mother died, Roger laughed and seemed totally relaxed. At the end of the evening, Gerald offered to share his couch with him, after declaring that he was obviously too drunk to walk home safely.

"Quite right," he replied. "Although I appreshiate your kind conshern, I shall call a taxshe. And return reshted tomorrow if I am invited."

Nancy was delighted. She had never seen this side of Roger. "Of course you're invited," she said, hugging him. "All the time. Always. And you'd better come back tomorrow because we're having boiled gammon and parsley sauce, your favourite."

In fact Roger turned up on Boxing Day morning without any sign of a hangover and laden enough to warrant kicking the front door gently, as he had not one finger free to ring the bell. Most uncharacteristic of the Roger Nancy had always known.

One of the things he was carrying turned out to be a 1920's roulette game which had belonged to his mother. This was set up on the table after lunch and they played for nearly three hours, with much ribaldry, accusations of cheating and incorrect arithmetic. The ball bounced right out of the wheel and rolled underneath the sofa and Nancy, her bottom stuck up in the air, had to poke it out laboriously with a ruler. Yes, it had been a very good Christmas.

*

With a sigh, Nancy took her mug of coffee into the hall and sat down on the stairs again. Her mobile phone played a muffled can-can in her pocket and Luke's voice broke into her reverie.

"Just finished my shift and I'm on my way provided nobody notices me sneaking out," he said.

"OK, darling. I might be upstairs so I'll leave the door on the latch," she replied.

Instead of going up, she finished her coffee and rinsed the mug. After unlocking the front door she sat down on the stairs again, unable to decide on the next task. She looked at the boxes piled in the hall. They were full of Roger's clothes, waiting to be taken to the charity shop. She was still finding it difficult to believe that he was really gone.

Her mind went back over the weeks to when she had that awful phone call from the police to tell her that Roger had been taken to hospital because he had suffered a heart attack. She drove there straight away, mindless of any speed limits, to find him barely conscious. Desperately trying to pour her strength into him, she held both his hands between hers, whispering into his ear for a long time. He rallied a little, obviously recognising her and trying to speak.

"My love-ly Nan. Be hap-happy. Ssstay Luke. He's goodmaan." Then he smiled at her and, in slow motion, his eyelids drooped shut and he was gone. Nancy called his name repeatedly and shook him but it was no use. A nurse appeared and gently removed her hands from his. Roger, in his own orderly way, had died.

*

When Luke came through the front door, he found Nancy still sitting on the stairs with tears streaming down her cheeks. He sat down beside her and wrapped her in his arms.

"Don't grieve so, my love," he crooned softly into her ear.

"You were with him and he knew it. He wouldn't like you to go on being so sad."

"It was his hat," Nancy said in a small, choked voice. "Look, on the top of that box there. His woolly hat that he wore on Boxing Day," and with a small sob, she turned and buried her face in Luke's chest.

Luke held her, rocking gently as if she were a distressed baby. Slowly the sobs lessened and became hiccups. His hands smoothed her hair and caressed the little dent in the nape of her neck while he murmured loving nonsense. Then gradually, the murmurs became punctuated with kisses, the caresses crept down onto her thighs and Nancy's hiccups became tiny, involuntary gasps of pleasure. She slid one step down the stairs, her skirt rumpling to expose stocking tops and bare thigh below her panties.

Luke too was now thoroughly aroused and guided one of her hands to the straining material covering his erection. Quickly she unzipped him, pulling down her panties with the other hand. As the silky material brushed his penis, Luke had to bite down hard on his tongue to prevent immediate ejaculation before her dampness enveloped him. In less than thirty seconds, they were both overtaken by an orgasm which seemed to go on forever.

In the stillness after the storm, they remained joined until their ragged breathing settled.

"Oh my love, my poor little sad, wonderful love," said Luke fondly, kissing her nose. "Now you've been raped on top of it all."

"Yes and on the stairs too," replied Nancy, fumbling in her pocket for a tissue. "Heaven knows what Roger would say."

"He'd be pleased as Punch," said Luke. "He loved you very much, you know."

"Yes, but not in that way. More like an older brother, surely?" said Nancy with a slight question in her voice.

"Roger and I became quite close over Christmas, darling," said Luke, holding her face gently in his hands and his eyes searching hers. "He was totally impotent and always had been. I told him that there was good treatment for this but he said he was content with the way things were and didn't want to change. So you see, he loved you very deeply in the only way that he could."

A single tear rolled slowly down Nancy's cheek and he wiped it away with his thumb.

"And I loved him," she said shakily, "I really did. And now he's left me all this. This house, his money, investments and all Aunt Marian's too. Whatever am I to do with it?"

"Be happy, that's what he wanted," said Luke decisively, pulling her to her feet, "and that's why he'd be so pleased that we made love on his staircase."

"Right," she said and pulled her skirt straight. "We'll have a cup of tea while we think what to do with all these boxes of clothing. His bedroom is now completely cleared out and tidy."

Roger's clothes presented a bit of a problem. They were expensive, mostly designer stuff and not much of it to Luke's taste, although they had been roughly the same size with a few adjustments. Luke thought that it might upset Nancy to see him in Roger's clothes, anyway. The problem was that they seemed too good for the Salvation Army, all wrong for Help the Aged and too posh and useless for foreign flood victims.

Then Nancy had a brainwave. She heard of an up-market boot sale held at a venue on the outskirts of London every Sunday and reckoned they could choose a fine day when Luke was not on call and make it a fun outing. The money they made could be used to buy something special for them both to remember Roger by.

Another problem was what to do with Aunt Marian's clothes. Roger had left her bedroom virtually untouched since she died, with the bed neatly made, her tortoiseshell brush and comb and make-up on the dressing table and wardrobe and chest of drawers stuffed full. It was slightly spooky, as if she had been on holiday and was expected home at any moment. The clothing was very good quality but far too mature in style for Nancy.

"Why not pack it all up and take it to the boot sale as well with Roger's things?" suggested Luke, feeling it was about time he had a brainwave too. "I could be in charge of the gents' department, as it were, and you the ladies'. It might be fun."

"You think Roger would approve of that also?" asked Nancy and agreed when she saw her beloved grinning and nodding like a fairground dummy.

*

They waited for a Sunday when the good weather forecast and Luke's time off coincided and left at five in the morning, so as to acquire one of the larger pitches. Roger's second vehicle, a roomy estate car with a roof rack, seemed appropriate for the task.

"D'you know, I'm sure you were right about Roger's approval," said Nancy, as they joined the queue at the gates of the venue. "It almost feels as though he's with us, cheering us on. We're going to do well between the three of us."

Do well they certainly did. They had packed two long clothes rails to hang things on and a small chest of drawers, as well as dozens of boxes full of neatly pressed clothing. At the last minute, Nancy had somehow found room for a full-length mirror as well. No sooner than they had set up their stall, they were surrounded by a crowd of people of both sexes, all trying things on. Luke found a new talent, wearing one of Roger's hats at a jaunty angle it had never known before and shouting encouragement to customers like a market costermonger.

At two o'clock they were exhausted, very hungry and there was nothing left except the rails and hangers. They had even sold the chest of drawers and mirror. A big hotel nearby was still serving a Sunday lunch buffet and as they ate they kept grinning at each other like idiots. One glass of sweet Sauternes wine each was allowed with their apple charlotte in order to toast first Roger and then Aunt Marian. The near empty estate car was driven home at a very sedate pace.

That evening in the mews they had a count up. It took some while as it was all in cash, coins as well as notes.

"I think I've got it right now, love," said Luke, eyeing the piles and stacks scattered all over the table and scribbling in his notebook. "We seem to have taken the magnificent sum of one thousand and three pounds twenty five pence."

"Really? That's incredible. Are you sure?" Nancy asked.

"Yup. Enough to get something to remember Roger by and give a bit to charity," said Luke.

Nancy said nothing, just looked down at her hands in her lap. "Mum was very upset when I rang her about Roger," she said eventually. "And she cried when she rang yesterday. First her sister, then her nephew. Her family's dwindling and she misses me. I've been wondering if I should go over. That money could pay the fare to Australia easily."

Luke felt as if his heart had taken the fast elevator down to the basement. She had plenty of money now. She could leave him, go to her parents, go anywhere in the world she wanted and with anyone she wanted.

"You must do whatever you think best, love, whatever makes you happy," said Luke with a calmness he was anything but feeling. "After all, it is your money and comforting your mother might be a better memorial to Roger than any painting or expensive artefact could be."

Nancy shook her head and tried to stifle a sudden yawn which appeared from nowhere.

"No big decisions now," she said. "It's been such a long unusual day and there's still so much to sort out at the house. I'm really tired, darling, but in a nice kind of way, I think. Take your ladylove to bed."

Wisely and with a sense of reprieve, Dr Luke Benson did as he was told.

* * *

– 8 –

There was one thing which was left behind when Nancy and Roger packed for the boot sale. Nancy had noticed it but by then it was getting too late. The car was already stuffed to capacity anyway. A few days later, she remembered it while giving Aunt Marian's bedroom a thorough clean up.

Tucked into the wardrobe, round the corner and almost out of sight, hung a long dust-proof, moth-proof and probably everything else proof clothes cover. Its slightly lumpy outline suggested that there was something inside. Nancy unhooked it and laid it on the neatly made bed. It was quite heavy. Carefully she unzipped the cover to reveal the contents.

The first thing that registered was the big, soft velvet collar and one rather beautiful and unusually shaped horn button below. The colour was green, reminding Nancy of the fresh spring leaves on the sage bush that she picked for cooking. Slowly she opened the coat and drew it from the cover, her hands relishing the feel of soft wool sliding against the satin lining.

"Oh, this is so beautiful," she murmured to herself.

Nancy wondered what it was doing in Aunt Marian's wardrobe, convinced that she had never seen her wearing it. Undoing the solitary fastening, she slipped the coat on, immediately feeling wrapped in warm, sensuous luxury. She did up the button and gave a little twirl in front of the mirror. The coat flared out from the shoulders like a cloak, then floated back again to envelop her body. It looked expensive and not at all old ladyish. With strange reluctance, she removed the velvet collar from where it was caressing her cheek and took the coat off. For some reason she couldn't explain, she was glad they hadn't taken it to the boot sale.

Mentally, Nancy gave herself a little shake. The room was filled with warm Spring sunshine and there she was, trying on a coat which was obviously meant for the depth of winter. Stupid woman, she thought to herself. Far more important things to do than fuss with coats. She put it back into its protective cover, hung it back in the empty wardrobe in solitary state and closed the door.

For a few weeks, Nancy had been feeling restless and, in a vague kind of way, worried. After Aunt Marian died, it took Roger a long time to sort her affairs out, even though her will was a simple one. Their solicitor, Mr Grant, was elderly himself, tall and thin with a slight stoop. His voice was dry and businesslike, he was economical with words and a smile was something rarely if ever bestowed on a client. Nancy found herself disliking contact with Mr Grant, so she failed to ask many questions when Roger died.

She simply assumed that Roger made out a new will immediately after his mother died. But it was a shock for her, as much of a shock as Roger's death. Nancy was not used to having a lot of money at her disposal, let alone being a property owner. Looking around the now tidy bedroom, she made a decision. She badly wanted to talk to someone who cared about her, so she would go home and ring her mother in Australia. Hang the expense, she could afford it now. It didn't occur to her that there was a perfectly good telephone right there downstairs in Roger's house, which was now her house.

*

As Nancy turned into the mews, she saw a familiar little white car parked outside and there on the doorstep was Gerald. He looked up with a cheery grin and came to hold the car door open for her, bowing low like a hotel porter in Park Lane. She scrambled out and kissed him, suddenly feeling very pleased to see him.

"I've been doing a spot of shopping and thought I'd drop by and cadge a cup of coffee if anyone was in. Didn't expect such an effusive welcome, though," he said, hugging her close.

"Come on in," said Nancy. "Luke's on duty today but I just decided to stop sorting out No. 33 and come home for lunch before I start throwing everything out of the windows."

Gerald followed her indoors, carrying a small shopping bag which he plonked on the kitchen table.

"You sound thoroughly fed up, love," he said, regarding her shrewdly over the top of his spectacles.

Busy filling the kettle, she said nothing for a moment.

Wisely, Gerald sat down and waited.

"Well yes, I am a bit," she replied finally. "D'you fancy sardines on toast with this coffee and then I'll tell you all about it?"

"Ooh yes. My favourite," said Gerald, "followed by this, your favourite," and after fishing around in the little shopping bag, he pulled out a sticky ginger cake.

"I love you, you know, Gerry," she said with a chuckle as she filled two coffee mugs. "I hope Luke doesn't mind. I feel much better already."

After they had demolished two rounds of toast each with a large tin of sardines and most of the cake, they carried second mugs of coffee to the sofa in the sitting room and sat down, Gerry with an almost imperceptible but contented burp.

"And I love you too," he said, "whether my son minds or not. So tell me what's wrong."

"Not exactly wrong," she replied after a moment. "More like uncertain, confused and a bit bewildered. I was toying with the idea of ringing my mother because I really need somebody to talk to, other than Luke I mean. Everything just seems to go round and round in my head without coming up with any sensible sounding answers."

"Australia's a long way away and your mum will probably be asleep in bed at the moment. I'm right here. Will I do?" Gerry asked, laying one of his large hands on her shoulder.

"Yes," Nancy answered briefly, resting her cheek against that comforting hand.

Then, suddenly feeling safe and relaxed, she let her woes pour out in a stream into Gerald's waiting ears. He listened without interruption and she eventually slowed down a little.

"I didn't want to worry Luke with all these petty feelings," she said. "He works so hard and he seems to have been just a bit preoccupied lately. I don't want to put him off me. Mum and Dad are so far away and I loathe old Mr Grant, even if he did look after Roger so well. Maybe I need a solicitor of my own now, who would also be an advisor, someone to talk to. D'you know anyone like that, Gerry?"

"Hmm, I do, as a matter of fact. My solicitor's also old but he has a son following in his footsteps. He's a very bright chap, clever but not cocky and full of shit. Alex Zeigfeld is his name, usually known as Ziggy. His father is a good friend of mine, socially as well as professionally. I could introduce you if you like."

"I like, I definitely like," responded Nancy, with enthusiasm born of relief. "As soon as possible would be good, before Luke gives up on me completely."

"Whatever makes you think he's going to do a stupid thing like that, girl?" asked Gerry.

"I feel he's put a distance between us in the last week or so," she said dismally. "Not physically but mentally, as if all this money and property has made a difference to how he feels about me. We're happy living together here but I somehow don't think he would want to marry me now. He hasn't even mentioned the future."

Her voice trembled and a single tear escaped and trickled down her cheek. Gently Gerry caressed it away and gave a great guffaw of laughter.

"Oh, aren't you the silly one. So that's at the bottom of at least some of this fretting," he said, tilting her chin up to look at him. "Now, listen to me. I know my son and he's totally potty about you. If he hasn't proposed properly yet, he's maybe scared you might turn him down now you've got all this wealth."

"D'you really think so?" Nancy asked hopefully, giving a little sniffle.

"Yes, I do. You are going to have to tell him how you feel and you'd better hurry up. I always wanted a daughter as well as a son and I've decided I want to have you as a surrogate for the longest time possible. I'm no Spring chicken, you know, and I've got arthritis. How am I going to play with my grandchildren if you two bugger about instead of getting on with it?"

It was Nancy's turn to laugh, which she did loud and long, hugging him delightedly. Then she looked at her watch.

"Luke's off duty in a couple of hours," she said. "How about staying to dinner? You can practise liking my cooking and I promise to talk about the future to Luke after you have found me a solicitor."

"It's a deal," replied Gerry. "You're on."

"I'll just put my car away in the garage and then get going on the food," said Nancy, a sense of purpose in her voice replacing the previous uncertainty.

Gerry grinned at her, heaving an inward sigh of relief. He was thinking how easy it was to get hold of the wrong end of the stick when you were young and in love. He had been much the same with Luke's mother.

A tired and rather dispirited Luke arrived in the mews a full two hours later, having had an unusually aggravating day at the hospital. An elderly patient had made a great fuss about the lowering of her knickers in order to have her abdomen examined. As she seemed to be in considerable pain, Luke was forced to call a lady doctor away from the children's clinic to do the job. It turned out to be a case of severe wind. Then a brawny young rugby player threw up on him while he was stitching a bad cut on his arm.

Poor Luke was feeling more dogsbody than doctor when he too saw the little white car and experienced an immediate lift of mood. He parked behind it and was greeted with the enticing aroma of chicken pasanda when he opened the front door.

"Hello, darling," Nancy shouted from the kitchen.

His father, who was sitting on the sofa with a glass of wine in his hand, gave him a wave and a cheery grin.

"What are you doing here making free with my wine and my woman, you unemployed reprobate?" asked Luke.

"Making free with your wine and your woman," came the reply, "although I didn't realise that you actually owned this delightful creature," said Gerry.

Nancy came out with another glass and enveloped as much of Luke as she could in a bear hug. He buried his nose in her hair.

"Sorry if I smell of curry," she mumbled.

"I smell of antiseptic and possibly puke, so I can hardly complain," said Luke. "Have I time for a quick shower?"

"Yes and if you're not on call tonight, take a glass of wine with you," said Nancy.

As he disappeared into the bedroom, he could hear Nancy's laugh and his father's responding chuckle and Luke suddenly felt a very lucky man. He was home.

* * *

– 9 –

Alan (Ziggy) Zeigfeld turned out to be quite a character. He was tall, well above six feet, almost uncomfortably thin and had rather beautiful long-fingered hands which inevitably moved in accompaniment to his voice when he spoke. Having a conversation with him was like watching a passionate and talented conductor working with a full orchestra. His wide, generous mouth seemed to smile a lot in time with flashes of light from the brightest blue eyes Nancy had ever seen. When asked later to describe him, she came up with just one word. Mobile.

True to his promise, Gerry lost no time making an appointment to introduce Nancy to Ziggy. Being Gerry, the scene of this meeting was a Chinese restaurant with a help yourself luncheon buffet. After the introductions, when Ziggy blanketed Nancy's proffered hand in both of his, they settled down with an enormous pot of jasmine tea which magically appeared. Nancy took to Ziggy immediately. She couldn't imagine anybody less like Mr Grant.

"Is it all right if I call you Nancy?" Ziggy asked.

"Of course," she replied. "As long as you haven't got two or three other clients called Nancy that you could muddle me with."

"No. I'll settle for just the one," he said solemnly.

"Before we get all businesslike, do you think we could eat?" asked Gerry plaintively. "I'm being driven mad by the odours that are wafting past my nose."

Nancy laughed and pushed back her chair. She had the feeling that there was no hurry or urgency to discuss things. The important part had already taken place. She felt safe in a way that she could not explain.

The three of them trouped up to the buffet tables, took warm plates and began an unhurried selection of a bit of this and some of that. Nancy was glad to see Ziggy pick up some chopsticks from a side table and followed suit. She had long ago discovered that good Chinese cooking tasted even better when with the use of the correct implements.

Ziggy put away an enormous amount of food for one so slim. He didn't pile his plate up but returned to the buffet more than half a dozen times, taking modest amounts and seeming to savour every mouthful as he ate. Nancy was greatly relieved to see this because it was the way that she herself always ate and often got grumbled at for being so slow.

"You know why a lot of silly people complain that they feel all full up after eating Chinese food, then hungry again an hour later? It's because they eat too fast and don't even taste it," opined Gerry, answering his own question and laying down his last well-gnawed spare rib bone with a contented sigh.

"They miss out all the satisfying business of selecting, cutting and chewing in the effort to fill the stomach as fast as possible. You can tell a great deal about people by the way that they eat. It's most interesting," added Ziggy.

"Yes, indeed," said Gerry with a smile, glancing at Nancy who was occupied with dipping prawns one by one into lemon sauce and popping them into her mouth with an expression of sheer bliss on her face.

Finally, all chopsticks were laid to rest on plates and they sat back contentedly. The restaurant owner, who knew Gerry quite well, wordlessly brought a fresh pot of tea as if expecting a minor discussion to begin, as it did so often in his restaurant.

Ziggy, elbows on the table, folded his hands beneath his chin, looked at Nancy and said simply, "Tell me."

So she did, all of it without pause or embarrassment, just as she had told Gerry before. Ziggy listened, quite still except for the occasional nose twitch and nod of his head.

His eyes never once left Nancy's face. When she got to the part where Gerry had told her about Ziggy, she trickled to a halt and had a long swig of Jasmine tea. Ziggy took advantage of the pause.

"Did your Roger have any other relatives he could have made the bequest to?" he asked.

"No, just my parents and me. We're all that's left really," Nancy replied.

"So there won't be anyone else popping up put of the blue to make a claim or similar nasty surprises?" Ziggy went on. "In my business that can be good news but it leaves you a little bit alone with your responsibilities. And what do you think Roger's wishes might have been for your future?"

"I think he wanted me to be secure and to marry Luke, Gerry's son. We've been living happily together for ten months now but haven't really discussed the future. And now I've got all this money, deed, stocks and shares and property to deal with and I don't know if it will make a difference to how Luke feels," explained Nancy, sounding a little wan for the first time since meeting Ziggy.

"If you, heaven forbid, should die tomorrow, then your next of kin, your parents, would automatically inherit everything unless you had made a will to the contrary. It seems to me that if Roger had wanted that, he would have made out his will to them in the first place. So the first thing to do is to bring me all the documentation connected with your inheritance and I mean absolutely everything so that I can get a full picture. Can you come to see me at my offices the day after tomorrow? I'm not far away," asked Ziggy.

"Yes, in the morning. I'm working in the afternoon," said Nancy.

"Right. Ten thirty then and don't forget to bring everything. Gerry will show you where my offices are. I must rush now."

With what was found to be one of his characteristic gestures, Ziggy stood up and covered Nancy's hands with both of his, then he was gone. When Gerry and Nancy got up to leave, they discovered that Ziggy had paid the bill on his way out.

In the following two days, Nancy spent time doing a chore she hated. She sorted all the paperwork connected with her new role as heiress into neat files and large envelopes, properly labelled. Luke was on evening duty so she saw little of him until the morning before her appointment with Ziggy when, without meaning to, she gave him a bit of a jolt by asking if she could borrow his large spare briefcase.

"Whatever do you want that for?" he asked, surprised. "Are you giving a lecture on facial exercises for perfect beauty, complete with complicated muscle charts?"

"No, silly. I'm going to see a solicitor with your father and I've got to take stuff with me."

"Good grief! Are you going to sue me – or something?" he asked cautiously.

"It's all this paperwork from Roger's affairs and about the future," Nancy murmured, her mind already on other things. "Can I have it, then?"

"Course you can. Help yourself. I'll see you later," Luke replied quietly and kissed her cheek, his heart filled with a an odd foreboding. It was as if she suddenly had a life which he knew nothing about and it was no help to realise that it involved his own father.

Feeling optimistic and oblivious of the disquiet she had caused in the mind of her beloved, Nancy carted the heavily loaded briefcase off to pick up Gerry.

*

"D'you want to come and sit in on the meeting?" Nancy asked him as she parked the car. "As my mentor and hopefully future father-in-law, I think you had better, don't you?"

"Certainly," replied Gerry. "Sitting around alone in parked cars is bad for the elderly, anyway. Ziggy is on the third floor but there is a lift and the view is superb. Come on, my girl."

Ziggy was waiting at the door to greet them as they came out of the lift and showed them into his office. He settled Gerry into a large leather armchair by the fireplace, telling him to sit still and keep quiet, much to Nancy's amusement. She was then led to a chair at Ziggy's desk and he sat down opposite, hands under his chin, blue eyes intent upon hers.

"Work first, coffee afterwards," he said. "Let me see it all."

He watched as she pulled envelope after envelope, file after file out of the briefcase and laid them in front of him. In silence he examined them and read them, placing each item in two piles on the desk. For a good ten minutes, the only sound in the room was the rustle of paper. Nancy felt not in the least bit troubled by the silence. In fact she felt oddly content, as if she had shifted a great burden onto other shoulders much stronger than her own.

Finally, Ziggy sat back in his chair, looked at her and smiled his wide smile.

"Well, we've certainly got quite a hefty package here, have we not?" he said. "I believe in things being handed down to the young. They have got to continue in life with all its surprises, difficulties and joys while the old are comfortably dead with no more worries. Roger has seen to it that you are well provided for the task."

"Except that I don't know how I should best deal with it all. It seems too much, kind of scary. Will you help me please?"

"Of course. You wouldn't be here otherwise and I should never hear the last of it from certain quarters if I refused," Ziggy replied, throwing a meaningful glance toward the leather armchair. "The first thing I shall do is make sure everyone has been properly informed that probate has been granted, that all your inheritance you now own and that it is in your name and not Roger's. This shouldn't take very long. I can do most of it by telephone and the rest online. However, it already appears to me that you are now a person of some substance."

"Oh. You mean rich?" said Nancy.

"Fairly, yes. I can handle a great deal for you but I'm not a financial expert. There are a large number of shares and bonds, that type of thing and you will need an accountant unless you prefer to deal with that side of it yourself."

"No. I've never owned any shares before and I'm not sure if my parents ever did. I think they just paid into pensions for their old age and never had any debts. I definitely need help in that direction," Nancy said firmly, a worried little frown creasing her forehead.

"If you don't know a suitable accountant," said Ziggy, leaning forward, hands beneath his chin, "there is one who works on the second floor beneath here. He is a trusted friend and we work together quite a lot. My wife and his are old friends, too. His name is Bernard Crossman, commonly known as Bernie the Books and I could introduce you as my client if you want."

"I want," replied Nancy, with a big smile of pure relief.

"Right. Can you come back the day after tomorrow, when I will have this lot sorted? I'll make an appointment for you with Bernie as well. Same time in the morning?"

Nancy nodded, still smiling as if hypnotised by the bright blue of Ziggy's eyes.

"Good. Settled then," said Ziggy, standing up. "Meanwhile, you have a think about what you want and have a chat with that man of yours about the future."

Nancy rose too and Ziggy came around the desk and clasped her hands. They both turned as a plaintive voice came from the big leather armchair.

"Is it all right if I speak now?" asked Gerry. "It's time for lunch and I'm hungry."

*

Nancy was in bed and fast asleep when Luke came off duty that night. In the morning, she cooked a late breakfast, full English, which she knew he loved.

"How did it go yesterday?" he asked, as he wiped up the last dribble of egg yolk with his toast.

She told him everything they had discussed, described Ziggy's offices and even the pizza that she had shared with Gerry.

"You seem pretty pleased about it all, anyway," commented Luke.

"Yes. I do feel better. I need an accountant apparently and Ziggy's arranged an appointment with one that he works with called Bernie tomorrow. He may be able to give advice about the best things to do financially as well as my tax returns. What d'you think, my love?"

Luke's heart sank. He didn't hear the word 'love'. It simply failed to register. First a jolly pal of a solicitor called Ziggy and now an accountant called Bernie joins in was what he was thinking. She's moving away from me, moving on and leaving me behind.

"You must do whatever you think best, consider whatever your advisers suggest. It's your life, your money," he said woodenly. "I must go in early today. I've got a mound of paperwork to deal with myself."

With that, Luke got up and took their empty plates into the kitchen. Nancy said nothing when he came back, shrugged into his jacket, picked up the car keys and kissed her briefly on the cheek.

"See you later if you're not asleep," he said and was gone.

Nancy sighed, watching him from the window as he drove away. So much for having a chat with her man about the future. She hoped Gerry was right about his son's true feelings for her. If he was, then Luke had a funny way of showing it.

As she didn't have to go to work for another couple of hours, Nancy decided to give Gerry a ring. After all, he had told her that he was always there if she needed him and Luke's attitude had confused her yet again. He seemed to her almost disinterested and reluctant to share any decisions that needed to be made.

After a long chat on the phone, on Gerry's advice Nancy went to bed early that evening. She was asleep, or appeared to be, when Luke got home. Next morning, she left early to keep her next appointment with Ziggy, first planting a loving note under the kettle for Luke to find when he came into the kitchen. He was still fast asleep in bed.

*

In Roger's house, in the back bedroom, in the big wardrobe in its protective cover, the coat was still hanging. A virgin, it waited to be worn properly for the first time instead of just being tried on or carried over the arm.

Alone in the dark, it waited patiently.

* * *

– 10 –

Bleary eyed and in his bath robe, Luke was slow to answer the doorbell. He got there in the end, hoping fervently that whoever it was would have gone away, taking whatever it was they were selling with them. He peered through the space that he initially made, then opened the door properly.

"Oh it's you, Dad," he said, surprised. "If you've come for Nancy, she's gone off to her appointment. I think."

"No, it's you I'm after, my lad, if you'll let me in," said Gerry, sounding a little exasperated and pushing past his son. "I want to have a serious talk with you and a cup of tea wouldn't come amiss while I do it."

"Sure. Yes. OK," said Luke, following his father into the kitchen.

It was Gerry who put the kettle on but Luke who picked up the teapot and found the note underneath. He was still trying to read it, albeit upside down, when his father carried the mugs of tea into the sitting room.

"What's the problem, Dad?" he asked after taking a good gulp from his mug.

"You are, at the moment. I've never before interfered in your adult life but I have the strong urge to do so now," said Gerry. "If I were Nancy's father and not yours, I would be asking you what your intentions are."

"Wh--at? What are you talking about?"

"The girl you live with, who loves you, thinks constantly about your welfare and needs, is always there for you and on your side. Yet when she is unhappy and has burdens she doesn't know how to cope with, it seems you couldn't care a jot."

"What's she been saying? She's said nothing to me."

"Nor to me, either," said Gerry. "It's what I've been seeing."

"She doesn't need me," said Luke. "She's got money now aplenty and Ziggy and somebody called Bernie running around after her, not to mention you of course."

Gerry stared at his son for a moment, then burst into loud laughter.

"Now what? What's the joke?" said Luke, a trifle grumpily.

"You're jealous. I really do believe you are jealous, you dunderhead. Ziggy and his mate are just giving Nancy professional help that she badly needs. She's in over her head with this big inheritance and she needs proper guidance. She also needs some understanding and emotional support and that should be coming from you. All you seem to have contributed is a ruddy great briefcase for her to cart the stuff around in. The girl loves you, heaven help her. Don't you understand that? I know you're busy but she needs you to be there for her. You. Not that distant housemate or doctor. You."

Throughout this tirade, Luke had been clutching the piece of paper which he had found under the teapot. In the ensuing silence, looking down at his lap, he read the words properly.

"So," said Gerry, "what are you exactly? Her boyfriend? Her live-in lover? Or the man she wants to go on loving come what may and give the rest of her life to?"

"I'm a dunderhead, that's what I am," said Luke miserably. "She went out this morning while I was still asleep and left this under the teapot. 'I need to rush but couldn't bear to wake you. You were so tired. I'll be back at lunch time and we need to talk, my love. Please be there.'"

His voice trembled as he finished reading and Gerry was filled with compassion for his son. He stood up and put an arm around Luke's shoulders.

"She's a lovely girl," he said. "She reminds me a bit of your mother, you know. Feisty, independent but loyal and always faithful to the people she loves. I think Roger saw that too."

"I do love her, Dad. Don't know where I'd be now without her," mumbled Luke.

"I know, boy. It's written all over you. So go for it. Pop the question and give me a daughter-in-law to love too before she gives up, runs away to Australia and gets mixed up with a sheep farmer. I must go now, it's getting late. Now, not a word to Nancy – I wasn't here, right?"

"D'you think she'll have me, even though I'm a dunderhead," asked Luke, as they went to the front door.

"Well, your mother and I did, so why not?" chuckled Gerry and hurried off with a cheery wave.

*

While Luke and his father were bonding, a few miles away Ziggy was introducing Nancy to his colleague and friend. Bernie Crossman was a truly large man, tall and far broader than the slender solicitor. Although he towered over Nancy, who was no shorty herself, she felt not in the least intimidated. In fact she found his deep, gentle voice soothing and comforting. She simply handed the big briefcase to him and relaxed into the chair he led her to.

"It's all there, I think," she said. "Everything my cousin had and gave to me, to do with banks, savings or investing. Ziggy says you will help me with the best way to manage it.

"Certainly I will," rumbled Bernie the Books. "Now, let's have a look," and he emptied the contents on to his desk.

After a while of shuffling through and a great deal of humming and muttering, Bernie leaned back and beamed his big smile at Nancy.

"Even from an initial glance, I can tell that this astute cousin of yours knew what he was doing financially. Unless something turns up to the contrary, my advice to you will be to leave these investments exactly where they are for the moment and they will provide you with a good, steady income," he said. "If you need ready cash, a few thousand has already been transferred into your own banking account and I can see two more instant access savings accounts here. How does that sound?"

"It sounds as if I don't have any money worries," replied Nancy happily. "Extraordinary."

"Good. If you want me to handle your affairs, I shall see to it that your tax bill is as small as it can be, of course, advise you how to make the most of it as things crop up and it will be a pleasure, I can assure you."

Nancy smiled at him and nodded emphatically. Ziggy had told her a little about Bernie. Apart from his wife and two sons, he apparently had only two other passions in life. One was for the game of golf and the other for figures. He regarded money as another game, valueless by itself but great fun to put to work and multiply.

Nancy felt comfortable with this attitude. She felt no awe at being rich and, in fact, a little worried that money might change the things that she did value. If, in the hands of this big, bluff man, the money could be used to enhance and stabilise those things that she did care about, then she was rich indeed and Roger was responsible. He would approve, she felt sure.

After another hour, Nancy left Bernie's office with an empty briefcase, safe in the knowledge that everything would be copied and that her affairs were now Bernie's problem. To whom they were no problem at all, of course, but a pleasure. She had to get home to Luke as soon as possible and drove with scant regard for the speed cameras.

The front door, to her surprise, was standing two or three inches ajar when she arrived.

"Luke?" she called. "Luke?"

There was no answer. She went into the living room and then stopped, gazing in amazement at an enormous bunch of flowers of every kind and colour imaginable which was lying on the table.

"Luke?" she called again and dropping her bag and the empty briefcase on the floor, went into the bedroom.

He wasn't there either but in the middle of the neatly made double bed was a huge box of chocolates, her favourite kind.

Mystified now and still calling, she went to the kitchen. Nothing. She was just about to go to the garage to see if he had locked himself in or something, when she heard a sound behind her and there he was.

"Luke. Where were you? I was getting worried," she said.

"I was hiding in the bathroom," said Luke sheepishly.

"Why? Why, darling?" asked Nancy. "What have you done?"

"Hardly any of the things I should have done and I'm so ashamed. When I read your note I was afraid you were coming back to tell me you were leaving me. So I bought you flowers and chocolates to see if I could change your mind."

"Of course I'm not leaving you," said Nancy, flinging her arms around him. "I'm trying to sort things out without worrying you because you're so busy. Oh, you dumkopf! I thought that you didn't like me being an heiress and having money. Do you know what a dumkopf is?"

"Yes. A dunderhead," said Luke solemnly. "I do love you so much."

"Well, that's one thing that doesn't make you a dumkopf or dunderhead or whatever. I'll get us an omelette because it's late and I'm starving. We can have chocolates for pudding," said Nancy, practical once more.

"Actually, I booked a table at the Fruits de Mer up the road in case the flowers and chocolates weren't enough," said Luke, still holding her. "Please, will you have lunch with me?"

Nancy did not need to be asked twice. Hand in hand they walked to the little restaurant and were greeted by Francois, the genuine French owner. Luke had once diagnosed his small daughter's tonsillitis on the spot when everyone else was saying that she just had a bad cold and Francois had never forgotten. They were given a table by the window and a small glass of sherry each with the menu.

Throughout the meal, Nancy explained everything that had taken place at her meetings with Ziggy and Bernie. Because she was so happy, her speech bordered on chattering, which was unusual for her. Luke listened, eyes roving her face while he took in all the facts.

"I'd really like you to come with me to meet them next time," she said, as they neared the end of the main course. "I should think poor Gerry must be bored stiff by now with the whole thing. Do you suppose you might be able to?"

"I'd like that and I couldn't get bored with you under any circumstances," said Luke, wiping his fingers on his napkin. "But there is one question I must ask."

"Go ahead," said Nancy. "I've been talking far too much."

Luke took her left hand, the one that was not occupied by the large king prawn which she had just dipped into mayonnaise.

"Please Nancy, will you marry me?" he said.

Nancy gave a small yelp, dropping the prawn halfway to her mouth. Luckily, it fell onto her plate and not the pristine white tablecloth.

"Are – are you serious?" she stammered.

"Never more so. I love you. To continue through life without you is unthinkable and I'm sorry it took me so long to realise it. Doesn't make a scrap of difference if you're an heiress or pauper," he said, trapping her other hand as well. "Please say 'yes'."

"Yes, oh yes!" Nancy yelled delightedly and their locked hands tipped her half full wine glass over.

There followed a mild commotion as Francois, who had been eavesdropping, rushed out from behind a screen. At the same time, the head waiter dived towards the table brandishing a clean cloth. They collided, of course, but

Luke and Nancy were too busy kissing to notice. That last prawn, mayonnaise smeared and now slightly dishevelled, was forgotten and enjoyed later by Francois' cat.

"We must ring my parents," said Nancy, when things had calmed down a bit and the pot au chocolat had arrived.

"No hurry. They probably guessed. I rang them this morning to ask your father's permission, being the old-fashioned lump that I am," said Luke.

"Very sweet old-fashioned lump. What did he say?" asked Nancy.

"Full approval. I know we only met a few times before they left for pastures new but I gather Aunt Marian and Roger had been singing my praises."

"I'm not surprised. The last thing Roger said to me was about staying with you," said Nancy with a little catch in her voice. "I'd like to tell your father though. I'd like to tell everybody really. I thought you didn't want me any more."

"Somehow I don't think I'm the only dunderhead and dumkopf sitting at this table," said Luke with a grin.

At this point, Francois reappeared with a bottle of champagne and some glasses. He sat down at the table and poured. Then the sous chef arrived and the waiting staff drifted over. They realised that the restaurant was now empty of customers. They drank and were toasted until Nancy felt she must burst with pure happiness. One of her toasts was to Roger, whose presence she was feeling strongly.

Finally Luke announced that they must go because he had to buy the ring to make it official. There was a slight argument when Luke tried to pay the bill and Francois only agreed if promised the sole responsibility of the wedding reception. Nancy and Luke wandered off in the direction of home in a state of euphoria.

"Could I have any ring I want?" asked Nancy, as they hove in sight of the mews.

"Of course you can. Did you have something in mind? One of the diamonds so cruelly rejected by Miss Elizabeth Taylor perhaps?"

"Not that keen on diamonds," giggled Nancy, who was very slightly tipsy. "No. But among Aunt Marian's jewellery in the safety deposit at the bank, there's a gorgeous nineteen thirties gold and aquamarine ring. I love it. Could I have that to wear instead of buying a new one? I'm sure she wouldn't mind."

"The bank's closed now," said Luke, peering at his watch. "I'm not on duty again until Monday. We'll go and get it in the morning, my love. Right now, we have some wonderful plans to make and some personal celebrating to do."

He kissed her for a long moment on the doorstep before going in. They didn't care a hoot that the council roadsweeper and rubbish picker had to skirt round them, muttering to himself about posh people having no shame these days.

* * *

– 11 –

The winds of change were blowing strongly and decisively. Yet they were benign winds and Luke, Nancy and Gerry too basked in their warmth. A lot of decisions took place about everyday things and important things. One question was whether Nancy wanted to carry on working, to which she hotly replied that she would always want to work, even if she became a multimillionaire.

She truly loved what she did. It was not just messing about with people's hair, nails or skin, a waste of time for girls who had nothing better to do, as some thought. Nancy had studied hard for her qualifications, going without pleasures like dances and cinemas to get there. Slowly she discovered a unique feeling of satisfaction when she managed to find a suitable way to disguise an ugly mole on a woman's face, so that even her husband who had previously been repulsed from time to time, couldn't find it.

It was things like that which made Nancy love her job rather than the good money she earned from doing it. What had first endeared her to Luke was the fact that he considered her job to be akin to his as a doctor. She tried to work at least four half days at the salon she was connected with, now proudly wearing her engagement ring. There were plenty of oohs and aahs from her regular clients who wished her well.

At a meeting with Ziggy and Bernie, who were fast becoming friends, the question of what to do with Roger's now uninhabited house came up.

"You could, of course, rent it out," said Bernie, after some consideration. "It could earn you quite a bit in rent these days."

"Hoo too? Hoo too?" asked the others in unison, sounding like a quartet of demented owls.

Phone calls and e-mails were zooming back and forth to the parents in Australia with the regularity of fireworks popping on Guy Fawkes night but no sensible suggestions emerged. This was probably due to the fact that everyone was so chuffed and happy about the engagement, they just talked about that. Practical matters took second place, although Luke did point out that his two-year stint at the General Hospital would finish in another five weeks and he had made no attempt to negotiate another term to follow.

Nancy was the only one to take this fact on board. She had forgotten that Luke's appointment to the hospital was not for ever. Without saying anything to the others, she slowly digested this information and wondered how an unemployed Luke would feel, even if newly married.

One morning, when the group met up for coffee and Luke had evening duty, Bernie came up with a small bombshell.

"Why don't you two love birds move into the bigger house and rent out the mews?" he said. "There's more room for two or more in the house and the mews would be relatively easier to rent."

Everyone turned to look at him, making him feel momentarily important.

"That might be a good idea," said Luke finally. "The house is just as close to the hospital and Nancy's work. The mews has become a fraction pokey for both of us. Also for having guests," he added, glancing at his father and remembering the bother of converting the sofa into a bed,

Silence followed. Then "Who...?" began Ziggy and Luke simultaneously.

"Now don't start all that again," said Gerry with some asperity. "Me, of course."

All heads now turned towards him, with several eyebrows raised enquiringly.

"This so-called sheltered flat I live in is getting up my nose a bit," Gerry went on. "When my wife died, I was in a state and a different frame of mind for quite a while. I wanted to be cushioned, not have to think too much and the sale of our house provided plenty of capital to add to my pension. But after some time, I woke up again and 'sheltered' became 'loomed over', you know."

The others were looking at him with the concentration of students at an important lecture. Luke felt a twinge of guilt for not realising his father's feelings sooner but Nancy thought she knew what was coming. Nobody said a word.

"I love that little mews place," said Gerry. "There's enough room for a person to breathe and I'd be fine on my own. I'll pay the going rent, of course."

"Oh, no you won't," said Luke and Nancy in chorus, then turned and grinned at each other.

"And I can still work, you know," Gerry persisted. "Yes, I'm supposed to be retired and may not be able to run up and down stairs like I used to but I'm still a good draughtsman. I can draw plans, earn a bit."

Luke had purchased a twenty-year lease on the mews property and had only been there for two of them. He knew the value was going up and it was well worth hanging on to.

"You can pay the ground rent, which is reasonable and the council tax, of course, but that's all," he told his father.

"Right. I only have to give a month's notice. They have a queue waiting to get in there but I can't think why," said Gerry, sounding quite cock-a-hoop. "I'll do it today, if you're sure.

"And," said Luke, turning to Nancy, "I'm happy to live in Roger's house if you are but on condition that I pay all the bills. All right with you, my love?"

Having successfully sorted out where everybody was going to live and with what rules, the group parted company to go their separate ways, feeling rather smug. Luke and Nancy decided to begin at once by moving furniture around, since neither had to be at work that day. Roger's old study, which was really meant to be a single bedroom, lacked a bed while having at least a cupboard or bookcase too many. A phone call to Gerry confirmed that he owned the divan bed in his apartment and obviously wouldn't need it in the mews. Problem one was solved.

Most of the other furniture in Gerry's apartment was built-in so a tall bookcase could be transferred from Roger's old study to the mews. Problem two was solved. It suddenly all seemed so easy. Nancy reckoned that everything became easy if you were happy and Luke said that she was probably right.

Being happy, Nancy's thoughts soon turned from furniture removal to the actual process of getting married. The telephone lines between England and Australia buzzed with activity again as she began to ring her parents almost daily. They came up with ideas and suggestions with growing excitement. Nancy was, after all, their only child.

The pattern that emerged was that everything seemed to be heading for the same time. Gerry's tenancy in his sheltered flat ending, Roger's house ready to live in and even Luke's term at the hospital coming to a close. It was as if fate was guiding things along to a climax or finished product. Nancy gave it a lot of thought. She was a great believer in things happening because they were meant to, part of a much bigger pattern of life.

Bernie had a long talk with her about inheritance. He explained that she would have to pay much more income tax than she had before, even though some of her money was placed in tax-free savings such as government bonds. Her next of kin, now her parents, would have to pay quite heavy death duties if she died intestate. Once married, however, something called a mirror will could be made between husband and wife to avoid this payment.

Although not in the least mercenary or greedy, Nancy did have good business sense. She disliked the idea of Roger's generosity to her being shared around in various government departments.

"Then I shall just have to stay alive until we get married at least, won't I?" she told a concerned and slightly anxious Bernie. "If you can get draft wills made out ready in advance, I'll talk to Luke about an early wedding date."

Bernie heaved a sigh of relief and apologised for being a little pushy. He blamed Ziggy, of course, for putting him up to it. Nancy smiled and kissed him on the cheek, making him turn quite pink. She felt lucky to have such good friends behind her. She chose a quiet moment at the mews the day before the move to Roger's house was to take place to talk to Luke.

"This is the last time we'll go to sleep in this bed and in this room," Nancy said dreamily, pushing her head further into the crook of Luke's arm. "When would you like to get married, darling?"

"At exactly the same time as you," he mumbled into her hair. "Other than that, I don't mind."

"What about our honeymoon?" she asked.

"Same thing," he replied. "Whatever and wherever you like. Really, I mean it. As long as I'm safely married to you, I could even enjoy exploring the Amazon in a rowing boat or maybe fighting off poisonous lizards in the jungle."

"Ugh!" shuddered Nancy, "How about facing overexcited new in-laws hugging and kissing you in the wilds of Sydney in Australia?"

"Fine by me. Can we go there in something bigger than a measly rowing boat? It is rather a long way and I shall be wanting to keep making sure that I'm properly consummated," said Luke, sitting up and looking at her with an earnest frown puckering his forehead.

"I've had a long talk with Mum and Dad," said Nancy, when she managed to stop giggling. "They did suggest that we could get married here first and then do it all over again in Sydney with them. I'd like that and I know they would love it."

"And so would I. Twice should make it doubly secure, no wriggling out of it for you, my girl. As long as we can go there on a big boat that has double beds or bunks, not crunched up in an aeroplane with toilets in tiny cupboards and people banging into you with trolleys full of gin and coffee. And I do not want them to know my profession. I have no intention of being woken up in the middle of the night to go and fiddle with other people's personal parts. Understood?"

Nancy just managed to say yes before being overcome once again by helpless giggles. If this was what marriage to Luke was going to be like, she couldn't wait. The first thing they did in the morning before moving house was to pay a visit to the registry office and book the day.

***

– 12 –

They had thought that planning a small wedding would be easy so they left it almost until the proverbial last minute. What they forgot was Luke's popularity at the hospital. His term of duty finishing was excuse enough but getting married at the same time was too much to take lightly. It seemed that everyone who had worked with him for longer than five minutes wanted to be a part of it, and Francois had insisted on providing the wedding feast as his gift to them.

Nancy and Luke were oblivious to the consternation they were causing. They loved being in their new home, enjoying silly little things like going upstairs to bed and eating meals in the back garden on warm, fine evenings. On being given the choice of where to sleep, Nancy plumped for Roger's old bedroom rather than the other double which used to be Aunt Marian's. She thought Roger would approve and they certainly slept well and deeply there. Luke forbade Nancy to sit on the bottom of the first flight of stairs. He said it always gave him an inappropriate erection, such as when he was just about to leave for work.

Surplus small furniture was winkled through the trap door into the loft to give more space and spare china and linen was packed neatly into boxes and trunks. Gradually, as the days passed, the house became home. Nancy's cooking became more adventurous and even stretched to baking her own bread. She told Gerry that she felt Aunt Marian was watching over her and giving her tips in the kitchen. Since many samples of her newfound skills came his way, Gerry heartily agreed with her.

The newly vacated mews was, in fact, ready for Gerry to move into before his apartment tenancy finished. He mentioned this to his son.

"Well, you are paid up until the end of the month," Nancy reminded him. "It'd be the waste of a couple of weeks' rent if you were to move now."

"Who cares?" said Gerry, thinking that Nancy had been greatly influenced by Bernie over money. "I'm totally fed up with all these old biddies buttonholing me every day about what's going to happen to the Book Club. You'd think I was the only mentally intact person in that place. I'd much rather be living in the mews and helping you."

So Luke cheekily borrowed an unmarked hospital van to move the single bed and all his father's personal possessions. Nancy stayed behind to cook a special meal for a housewarming party. The bagatelle board and the roulette wheel were reunited and not just one but two bottles of champagne appeared alongside the wine.

Nancy invited her friend Dinah, who owned the beauty salon where she worked and was divorced. She planned to ask her to be the other witness at the wedding and as Gerry would be sort of best man, it seemed a good idea for the two to meet socially beforehand.

The little dinner party turned out to be a huge success. Gerry and Dinah found almost instant common ground over Edward Lear and John Betjeman. As the evening wore on, they even made up a few fairly passable limericks of their own until they drew a blank at Nancy only rhyming with fancy. Crispy duck and a strawberry meringue went the way of all good food and Luke finally assembled the old roulette wheel, the bagatelle board and then declared the Mews Casino open. It was reminiscent of their last Christmas and just as much fun.

The actual wedding was booked for half past twelve on the last Tuesday of the month. Francois became anxious about the numbers he should expect and Luke had to explain that although it was only a small affair, all the people from the hospital would have to come along in dribs and drabs as they came off duty. It would probably stretch over the whole afternoon into evening. He suggested a selection of cold finger food, nothing hot. Francois was determined to produce the cake of the year and wanted to know Luke and Nancy's favourite flavour. The air of excitement grew daily.

Luke came home one day with the news that the doctor who was expected to replace him would arrive three days after the wedding and wanted to rent a house furnished for the first three months at least, while he got settled. He was married with twin children, a boy and a girl of four years old. His name was Gareth Evans and he came from Aberdovey.

"Shall I suggest our house?" Luke asked Nancy. "It's plenty big enough and we can get all our personal stuff out by then."

"Don't forget we'll be getting on that big boat on the Saturday, to disappear over the horizon to Australia. I suppose we could stay the night before in a hotel near the docks. Has this new chap got references and things?" asked Nancy.

"Of course he has, you chump. Anyway, I expect the terrific two will be sorting out the legal and financial side of it. But it is your house after all, not mine, so it's your decision," said Luke, without any rancour.

Nancy looked at him, head on one side, considering for a few moments.

"If it's OK with you, then it's OK with me," she said. "Let's heave it over to Ziggy and Bernie and get on with all our packing."

*

The day of their wedding dawned fine and warm, the haze on the horizon promising real heat for later. Luke had stayed the night with his father in the mews, after sharing two good bottles of vintage burgundy with rare fillet steaks, followed by brandy.

They talked of many things into the early hours, then slept like babies until the alarm roused Gerry at half past eight. Much the same had taken place at the other house with Nancy and Dinah, except that they indulged in king prawns and Gewurztraminer and Dinah grew a fraction lachrymose about her own failed marriage.

Midday found the four of them walking to the registry office. Luke felt that there was a dreamlike quality to the whole journey. There was a deep happiness and contentment that he had never felt before, not that he could remember anyway, and he knew that it was the same for Nancy. Afterwards, with full hearts, they wandered off to the Fruits de Mer. Love appeared to be catching. Nancy noticed with a smile that Dinah's hand crept into Gerry's as they walked along.

Francois had excelled himself in an effort to please his most favoured customers. By request, the cake was lemon and ginger, unusual but quite splendid in the centre of the table. The rest of the buffet was explained by Francois as a special exercise and practice for his culinary prowess. All this was relayed in perfect French and had to be painstakingly translated at length with much gesturing and noisy kissing of the air. One bite of each dish was all it took to confirm that the state of excellence coming from the kitchen was no mere boast.

A reception committee of about a dozen from the hospital were already there, some with stethoscope necklaces, some even in green scrubs but all determined to be first to kiss the bride and supply robust hugs and backslaps to their lucky departing and much to be missed colleague. Ziggy and Bernie arrived with their wives who, Luke declared, were almost as beautiful as his and also a bevy of well-behaved and attractive teenage children.

Gerry was surprised by a preponderance of well-coiffed and fashionable looking ladies who suddenly appeared. He wondered where his son could possibly have met all these lissom creatures until he realised, with some relief, that they were actually his new daughter-in-law's clients. When

Dinah began to introduce him, he suddenly found himself the centre of attention and began to enjoy it.

In one corner of the restaurant, a trio of musicians were playing softly, led by an accordion. Nancy closed her eyes and could easily imagine herself on the streets of Montmartre. On the terrace in front, an extraordinary little man wearing a beret was sitting at an easel surrounded by paints and brushes. He made lightning sketches of the guests which bore an uncanny likeness, although in a cartoon fashion. He looked rather similar to Toulouse Lautrec, which added to the romantic atmosphere.

Gerry was called upon to make a speech, which rather took him by surprise. He did quite well with a bit of whispering and prompting by Dinah. The toasts were toasted and the cake finally cut and declared the most delicious ever. Francois insisted that a large portion be packed away in an airtight tin to be carried to Australia. He wished Nancy's family to taste the best before the second party took place all those miles away. Luke did wonder if the Customs and Excise people would allow the importing of edible goods whatever the reason but he wisely said nothing. Francois had spared nothing with his generous gift and deserved his little bit of conceit.

As dusk fell and Luke and Nancy decided that all the guests who were coming had come and gone, they thanked Francois with much cheek kissing and left for home, hand in hand and very happy.

The accordion trio followed them, still playing, with a handful of remaining guests who covered the front step of the house with confetti. As soon as Luke and Nancy had waved everyone goodnight and closed the door, they put a telephone call through to Australia.

"Hello. This is your son-in-law, Luke Benson," said Luke solemnly to Nancy's mother, who answered the phone. "My wife is here and would like to speak to you."

Tiny squealing sounds were coming from the phone as he handed it over to Nancy, who immediately began to chatter into it like a deranged parrot, even though she had spoken to her mother almost every day.

"We had such a lovely marriage and party, Mum. I wish you both could have been there but we've got lots of photos and we'll be with you in a few weeks," she said, slightly tearfully.

"Think about what will be waiting for you here, darling," said her mother. "You'll be able to do it all over again only a bit different. Enjoy your ship's cruise honeymoon meanwhile."

Nancy reluctantly put the phone down and kicked her shoes off.

"They seem to have our second wedding arrangements all planned. I suppose this time rather than hospitals and hairdos it'll be didgeridoos, aboriginals, a barbecue and loads of people wearing hats with corks on them all waiting to kiss the bride," she said.

"Oh, no. I'm not having my wife carted off by some feckless Crocodile Dundee character into the bushes," said Luke, with an attempt at belligerence. "Come here, my love, and be consummated, properly and safely married."

Determined to be an obedient wife from the start, Nancy did as she was told.

* * *

– 13 –

Helen Evans wasn't just happy with her new home, she was delighted, even though it mainly contained someone else's stuff and furniture and might not be permanent. It had a good feel about it and she actually liked the furnishings, particularly the old Victorian things. Somebody who had lived here, she reckoned, had very good taste. It reminded her of her parents' cottage in Treorchy, where she had grown up.

One of the things she revelled in was the space, the opposite of the rather cramped bungalow they left behind in Wales. There was room for her big sewing machine which had languished in the garage before and was hardly ever used. Now it had pride of place in one of the small bedrooms and she was able to rediscover the many magical things that she could do with it. Helen even allowed herself to wonder if the owners would like her to design new drapes and curtains for the house. Soft furnishing was her main interest rather than clothing.

The children could run riot, almost get lost inside on rainy days. Although the garden was small, as with most town houses, it was enclosed and safe. This was important to Helen as Ivor, who was the nosey one given to exploring, would always find his way out of anywhere with the smallest of openings or climbable barriers. Jane was more sedate but not much. She adored her brother and would follow him anywhere without fear or question.

Sometimes Helen missed the cry of the gulls wheeling over the mudflats of the estuary and the outline of the distant mountains through the early morning haze. The bungalow had been only steps from the beach too and when the tide was very low, she and the children went down with buckets to collect mussels. If they were lucky, they had moules marinière for dinner a couple of times in a month.

But there were compensations. Gareth getting the job of his dreams at a busy hospital like the General, for instance. It wasn't just the salary, although that was three times the one he had received in Wales. It was the experience and the responsibility which had given him the confidence to recognise what a really good doctor he was. Helen thought that sometimes he seemed like a completely different person. Not that she minded, not one bit, because he was so obviously happy. And if he was happy, so was she and so were the children.

They found a good nursery school for Ivor and Jane. It was not far away and syphoned off some of their energy in the mornings, leaving Helen free to hone her sewing skills. She also found that she was more and more drawn to the roomy, old-fashioned kitchen with its walk-in pantry, cool marble shelves and hidden nooks and crannies for storage. She found a whole set of cookery books and began something that she had never bothered with very much before, gourmet pastry cooking. Her mother had taught her when very young to make traditional bara brith and Welshcakes but now she pored over recipes for treats she had never heard of.

These days, Gareth frequently came home to a house redolent with the smells of baking. He reacted like the Bisto Kid, nose in the air, following the scent to the kitchen. An attempt to snaffle a taste of whatever it was that was cooling on a rack usually earned him a slap on the wrist.

"Now you leave that alone, my cariad," Helen would scold. "It's not cool yet and it's for pudding later."

Gareth didn't mind. He was happy and just glad that she had taken up such a rewarding new hobby rather than Bingo or Chinese martial arts. His only concern was that it seemed to have become almost a compulsion or addiction with her.

Ivor and Jane were happy too. They loved going to nursery school and making lots of new friends who frequently came to tea because Mummy made such lovely cakes. They also loved having the run of the great big house and it did seem very big to them. Jane was especially fond of the staircase, a novelty to her, which she bumped down quite fast; step by step on her bottom. Going up was a hands and knees job and rather slower, usually side by side with her brother in a kind of slow motion race.

In the bungalow the children had bunk beds, one above the other in their tiny room. Ivor climbed the ladder to the top bunk with his sister safely ensconced below. This was in case she ever needed protection, of course, which he felt he could best provide from above. Although they could easily have had one of the small bedrooms each in the new house, this idea was immediately shouted down to the point of real tears. There was no separating these two, at night or even in the bath. Helen did not anticipate either sets of grandparents wanting to come and visit too much as both tended to dislike travelling outside their beloved Wales. So Ivor and Jane slept in the big comfortable double bed in the big spare bedroom.

Every night when Helen tucked them in, she smiled to see the two innocent little heads on their separate pillows at separate sides of the wide bed. As she looked lovingly at their sleepy faces, she did wonder what would happen when they grew older and the innocence became awareness. However, that was another bridge to cross in the future. Right now they were happy. They were all happy.

While the children were at nursery school, Helen used her free time not just to bake and sew but to do all the domestic chores. Except, of course, on the odd morning when Gareth was not on duty. There were far better ways to occupy their time together then.

On this particular morning, as she was on her own Helen decided to give the children's bedroom a really good spring clean. She gazed around it with something akin to despair. Every book they possessed seemed to be lying open on the bed, as if they had indulged in a giant reading binge the night before and fallen asleep in the middle of it. The rather pleasant beige carpet had sprouted a strange crop of tiny toy cars and trucks, with the odd doll on its back, staring vacant-eyed at the ceiling above.

Helen opened the doors of the low cupboard under the window as wide as they would go and began gathering up armfuls of toys, stacking them tidily on the shelf inside. She knew it wouldn't stay that way for long but hoped that her offspring would get the idea sooner or later.

The large pine coffer they called the dressing up box was a different matter. It was stuffed so full that the lid gaped open with small bits and pieces hanging out, rather like a greedy frog grinning with its mouth too full of food. Helen rearranged the contents and pressed them down until the lid closed. A gold crown with red stones like rubies lay on the floor beside what was meant to be a smoking pipe but looked more like a long spoon. She had made it for Ivor during his first week at nursery school when the children had to come dressed as someone famous. For some reason, Ivor had insisted on being Old King Cole like the picture he had seen in one of her own nursery rhyme books that she had kept.

Unable to face another battle with the contents of the dressing up box, Helen picked up the crown and pipe and left them on the lid. She looked around the now fairly tidy room with some satisfaction and turned her attention to the laundry. Gareth had fixed a much lower hanging rail in the big double wardrobe since the children had expressed a wish to dress themselves. Both parents agreed this was something to be encouraged.

Helen carried in the newly ironed clothing and began to hang it up, right side for Ivor and left side for Jane with shoes all lined up underneath. As she placed the last of Jane's dresses at the end of the row, she noticed something tucked into the corner hanging from the higher rail. It was a zipped-up cover with something inside. Carefully, she eased it from its rather awkward position and laid it on the bed.

She was sure she did not know this opaque dark grey cover and assumed that it must have been left by the owners of the house.

Overcome by curiosity, Helen started to undo the zip which was heavy and rather stiff. Finally, something soft and green was revealed and she took it off the hanger. It was a lady's coat and, thought Helen, one of the most stylish and beautiful that she had ever seen. She undid the single horn button which held it together at the top and the lining whispered like silk as she caressed it. The sudden desire to try the garment on and, if it fitted, to wear it was irresistible. She remembered the owners' solicitors saying that anything not required for use in the house could be put away in the loft. The crescent shaped button beneath the shawl of the collar seemed to beckon. So perhaps...

At that moment the telephone rang, on the land line which was downstairs. Helen dropped the coat on to its cover and hurried to answer it.

"Oh hello, Mam, I thought it might be you. Bore da. How are you and Dada today?"

Helen had always been close to her mother and since moving from Wales had kept in touch by telephone two or three times a week. Her father was busy trying to become computer literate and so be able to make contact by magic e-mail but he had never liked machines other than a motor car, so progress was slow.

"Your Dada is very ill in bed, unable to do more than read the paper," Helen's mother informed her. "He has a cold of the runny nosed type, you see."

Helen did see and she laughed, an immediate picture of her big, tall bearded father laid low invading her mind. A fairly long commiserative chat followed.

"Oh my! I'd forgotten the time," Helen said finally. "I must go and collect the children from school. Love to Dada. Now don't kiss him. Gareth says that's the main way colds are spread. Ring you on Sunday."

She rescued her handbag from the depths of the sofa, snatched the car keys from their hook behind the front door and was gone.

*

Ivor and Jane were on great form. They had been playing charades and chattered like magpies all the way home. A thin drizzle had begun to fall, so letting off steam in the garden was out of the question. They made for the stairs straight away, going up on all fours as usual. Helen watched the two little round bottoms disappearing, Ivor two steps above Jane of course, and smiled to herself, thinking how lucky she was. She decided she had time to bake brownies and meringues for pudding that evening.

The children scampered into their bedroom and Ivor stopped when he reached the bed.

"All our things are gone," he said. "Where's my cars?"

"Mummy's been doing tidy. P'raps somebody's coming to see us," said Jane.

Ivor grunted crossly, then caught sight of the coat lying on the bed.

"Whass this?" he said, picking up a sleeve.

"Spect it's a new blanket," said Jane doubtfully.

"No, it's not. It's a robe, a royal robe. It's got fur on it, look," said Ivor, stroking the coat's velvet collar and sounding enthusiastic again. "It's for me and there's my crown."

He had spied his things on top of the coffer and rammed the cardboard crown down on his head. Tugging at the coat, he managed to free it from the cover.

"We're going to a big parade," announced Ivor importantly, trying to drape the heavy coat around himself. "You can be my pageboy and hold the bottom bit out of the mud. Come on."

The coat was, of course, far too big but he got it round his shoulders and tied the sleeves round his waist.

"Bring me my pipe, slave pageboy," he said imperiously and Jane obeyed.

"Now, pick up my robe and follow," he continued, thoroughly into the part by now.

Jane struggled with the folds of the coat all over the floor, trying to gather it into her small arms. Ivor started to strut down the passage and she could hardly keep up with him. When he passed the head of the stairs and turned, Jane dropped her burden then fell on top of the pile.

"You are the most clumsy pageboy I have had," said Ivor sternly. "Get up at once. The parade is beginning without me."

Poor Jane tottered to her feet and picked up the coat again as best she could.

"Sorry, your majesty," she said fearfully, knowing how to play her part too. "We must hurry."

As they marched on back the other way, the sleeves of the coat detached themselves from Ivor's waist and trailed on the floor. They approached the head of the stairs and Ivor suddenly got his feet entangled in them. He fell forward at full length and hit his head on the newel post. There was a nasty sound, rather like a walnut put in the nutcrackers at Christmas.

Still holding the bottom of the coat, Jane came to a halt and looked down at her brother.

"Now who's clumsy? We really will be late now. Come on, get up," she said and prodded him with her foot.

Ivor didn't move or speak. Jane dropped the coat and knelt down beside him. She shook him and pulled at his hand. She bent over and put her lips to his ear.

"Open your eyes," she said loudly but Ivor didn't even twitch.

After a while, Jane got up and bumped down the stairs slowly, following the baking smells to the kitchen.

"Hello, my Janie girl. Where's Ivor, then?" asked Helen, knowing he was never far behind.

"Asleep," answered Jane, climbing on to a stool.

"Asleep? But you both had a nap at school, didn't you? He isn't asleep again surely."

"He is. He's asleep. I can't wake him up," said Jane, a little resentfully.

"Where is he? Is he in bed?" asked Helen, suddenly alert.

"No. He's on the floor upstairs. I can't wake him up," repeated Jane with a big sigh

"Come and show me, darling," said Helen, her spatula falling with a clatter.

Gathering her daughter from the stool, she took the stairs at a run. Her heart almost stopped at the sight which greeted her on the landing. Like Jane had done, she knelt down beside the little boy and took his hand.

"Ivor. Ivor, wake up," she pleaded.

Realising that his hand was totally limp, she gently turned his head and saw the swelling on his forehead. One eye was half open and the other closed. There was no response.

"Janie, go quickly and get Mummy's mobile phone from beside her bed. Hurry."

Without a word, the little girl obeyed and returned within seconds. Helen took her phone and, trying to stop her hand from shaking, she dialled 999 for the first time in her life.

* * *

– 14 –

Sister Kate Malone was as Irish as her name. She couldn't have been more Irish if she had worn a green suit with a pointed cap and sat around on a toadstool all day. She was born in Waterford, then the family transplanted to England when she was ten years old, yet this did nothing to dampen her Irishness.

When she was nine, Kate had an accident. She was riding her bicycle far too fast down the gravel driveway at school. In her anxiety to get home early that day, she lost control, fell and then skidded along several feet in the gravel. The bike was relatively undamaged but unfortunately Kate landed front downwards and it took the doctor three hours of careful patience to remove the tiny stones in her face and arms.

Painkillers helped during the following weeks of healing but she was left with a complexion that was impossible to hide. Her parents had a little money on arrival in England but certainly not enough to consider expensive plastic surgery, even though her father did get a good, well-paid job in the building industry very quickly. So Kate studied hard at school and learned to keep the worst side of her face away from people. As she grew into her mid-teens, make-up became the norm and she was skilful with it but the furrows and dents still showed.

Like all young girls, Kate dreamed of one day meeting her own prince to marry and then have a baby or two to love. But the boys she met, even at church, were only interested in beautiful and undamaged princesses. They did not notice Kate's lovely eyes, which were unable to make up their minds whether to be green or blue and so became a wonderful shade of turquoise. Neither did they notice the lustrous russet curls of her hair or her ready smile and kindness. They just saw her poor, pitted face, gave an inward, not always invisible shudder and turned away.

When she was twenty, her parents suggested that, as she seemed to be so fond of children, she should train to become a professional nanny. After a few semi-unsuccessful tries at being a shop assistant, a waitress and an office 'girl Friday', Kate thought this might be a good idea. Then she remembered the old music hall song that her grandma used to sing.

"Other people's babies, that's my life.
Mother to dozens but nobody's wife"

After humming it for a moment or two to be quite sure, Kate regretfully told her parents, who she knew were only trying to be helpful, that she thought permanent nannydom wouldn't suit at all. She was only twenty and still had hope. The dream was still there, alive and well and living in her big, loving-heart.

Two more years of shops, cafes and offices and Kate decided to train as a nurse. She found she was good at it and passed her exams with flying colours. She felt needed in a world where one's physical well being mattered more than physical looks, a world where scars, contusions and looking slightly odd were somehow commonplace. Once she had qualified, time and again she found she was drawn to the children's wards. So Kate began to specialise and that was how she came to be in charge of the I.C.U. for children in the General Hospital. At the age of 42, she realised that her prince was just part of a dream, along with the rest of it. It was too late and her destiny must lie elsewhere.

"Now, Laura, if you're to become a proper nurse you mustn't stand around all day just thinking. Particularly in a room like this one. Have you checked the machines? All the dials?" Kate asked the young girl standing next to the bed.

Laura jumped guiltily when she saw who had just come in.

"Yes, I have, Sister Malone. Everything just moments ago. I was only thinking that he looks a little bit pinker today. Not quite so pale," she said nervously.

Kate looked down at the child in the bed with all his attachments to the machinery. A little pinker, indeed? Well, perhaps he was but it was going to take more than a bit of colour in the cheeks to arouse this poor little chap.

"Have his parents been?" asked Laura

"Been? Do you not know who his parents are? Sure, how could you and you only here five minutes. He's our own Doctor Evans' little boy but perhaps you don't know who he is either?"

Laura was somewhat taken aback by this passionate speech from her superior and only managed to reply with a shaky "Oh."

"Well now, you soon will know him for he pokes his head around the door every hour at least or whenever he can. They live not far away and the ambulance brought the boy straight here and his father was on duty in casualty. 'Twas a terrible shock for him, to be sure."

"How did it happen?" Laura ventured, sensing that Kate was in the mind to talk.

"He was playing and tripped over, hitting his head on the stair post. The X-rays show no fracture but he's in a deep coma. He is breathing for himself but that's about all. The rest we have to do for him until he wakes up."

"How long will that be?" asked Laura.

"Who knows. It could be tomorrow or next week or month. I believe there have been cases where the patient was unconscious for years and suddenly awoke feeling fine. Meanwhile the machines and the boy must be watched over all the time and never left alone. It's all we can do. And maybe pray," Kate added with a sigh.

She looked down at the sleeping child and tried to imagine the despair this wait was causing for his mother and father.

"Oh, poor little boy. It's awful," said Laura in a trembly voice near to tears.

"Now then, stop that. Your crying is not going to help one bit," said Kate firmly. "Go now and have your break and come back refreshed to continue your watch. I'll stay here. Remember you must be alert when you're in here and notice everything. Blowing your nose and weeping will just make you incompetent. Only have twenty minutes now."

"Yes, Sister Malone," said a subdued Laura and left the room. Kate knew she was being hard on the girl but she would never make a nurse if she let her feelings get the better of her. If she herself let go of control, she could easily pick the child up and hold him close to try desperately to force life into the little body and probably kill him in the process. Instead, she did the only thing she could do at that moment. She watched and prayed, sitting close to him and holding the limp hand in both of hers.

The door opened and Helen appeared, followed by Jane clutching her skirt.

"Good day to you, Mrs Evans. You're early," Kate greeted her. "There's nothing to report yet,"

"No, don't get up. I'll sit on the bed for a minute, among all the pipes," said Helen. "Funny how he always wanted me to sit on the bed when I read to them."

Kate could tell that the mother was close to tears as her memories pulled at her yet again. Jane had gone round to the far side of the bed and was leaning over her brother, softly calling his name and kissing him.

"Was there no nursery school today, Mrs Evans?" asked Kate.

"She won't go without him," Helen answered in a low voice, glancing at her absorbed daughter. "She hasn't been for three weeks since it happened. They've always been so close. I don't know what to do for the best."

Kate reached out and covered the younger woman's hand with her own, feeling a deep compassion for her.

"Will we go and sit in the garden where we won't be sturbed and eat them?"

Jane experienced a slight frisson of thrill, as if part of a onspiracy, something she hadn't felt far a long while. She odded and they set off once again for the garden.

"When will Ivor wake up?" she asked suddenly. "He *will* wake up, won't he?"

"Of course he will," Kate replied. "It could be soon or it could be longer. It's already been three weeks, I know, but his poor little head has had a very bad shaking with that big bang so it has to sleep and recover. The mending takes time, sometimes a long time."

They reached the quiet little garden behind the hospital chapel, went through the gate and sat down on a bench under the chestnut tree. Kate broke open Jane's chocolate packet for her and then opened her own, taking the first finger and biting off the end.

"Oh, this is a treat, is it not?" she said after munching for a moment and noticing that the little girl hadn't begun.

"It's all my fault. I did it," stuttered Jane suddenly. "It's my fault he can't wake up," and a great tear dripped down on to her chocolate.

"That can't be so," said Kate with surprise. "How could that be true?"

"Well, I was supposed to carry his robe behind him because we had to hurry and I was his slave but that coat was too big. I couldn't manage it and it got tangled and he fell over it. He wouldn't have if I'd carried it properly."

The last words were choked out in a sort of hopeless wail and another tear splashed down. Kate's heart was torn and she gathered Jane into her arms and held her on her lap, rocking gently. As she did so, a memory from long ago crept into her mind, a memory of being blamed for something unfairly.

"'Twas not your fault, my little love," she said, as Jane's sobs began to subside into hiccups. "You were doing your

"Sure, you look worn out with worry, my d[ear]. I think it might help if I had a little word d[…] Sometimes they do listen to someone not so close.["]

Helen turned to look at her with eyes filled with [tears.]

"Would you, oh would you? You do seem t[o have a] special way with children. She likes you, I know."

Kate patted Helen's hand and nodded. She got u[p,] finger to her lips and moved round the bed. The roo[m was] silent except for the hum and occasional click of the support machinery. Softly, Kate called the little girl's n[ame.] Jane looked up at her, eyes dull with sadness.

"Will we be going along to my office just now?" K[ate] whispered. "I did hear someone was putting a few of the little chocolate wafer things there for me. Shall we go an[d] look? Mummy will sit with your brother for a while."

Hesitantly, Jane put her hand out and nodded. Wafers were her favourite. Ivor wouldn't mind because he didn't like them.

"We'll not be long now," Kate said to Helen with a tiny wink of her eye and they left the room, quietly closing the door.

Down the corridor they went, the child confidently stepping out with her hand safely enclosed inside Kate's. At last they reached the office and Kate started to rummage on her desk. Jane stood patiently watching with solemn eyes.

"Now where would they have put them? Certainly they would not have eaten them for themselves knowing my particular fondness," murmured Kate.

She opened the top drawer of the desk, then stood back with a smile.

"Well now, if they haven't hidden them to worry me!" she exclaimed. "Come here and see, Jane."

The little girl moved forward and there in the drawer, half beneath a sheaf of papers, were two bright pink packets of chocolate wafers. Kate gathered them up, giving one to Jane and keeping the other, closed the drawer and took her hand again.

job properly. I think it was the fault of that coat. It tripped your brother up and brought him down."

"How? You mean it deribe... delimber..."

"Yes, deliberately," said Kate. "It made him fall."

"Why? Why would it do a wicked, nasty thing like that and when I was trying so hard to hold it?"

"Perhaps because it was jealous or feeling mischievous or maybe because it is just plain bad, that coat, and didn't want to be held. I believe that there are bad things, you know, as well as bad people, sort of born that way or made that way from their beginning. I had something like that when I was no bigger than you are."

As the child gazed up at her trustingly, the memories came flooding back to Kate, things she had not thought of for many years. She had been indeed only four when she was given the chair. It was a small three-legged chair made from the wood of a pine tree which a neighbour, Tom O'Leary, felled. Uncle Tom, as she called him, gave it to Kate as a birthday gift and she loved it. Her mother told her to take great care of it and she promised she would.

The first time she sat on the chair, it tipped her off, spilling her milk on the rug and throwing her last morsel of cake into the fireplace among the coals. Her mother admonished her for not sitting properly in the middle.

"But I was, Mama, I was truly," she stammered, and so she was. She didn't sit on the chair again immediately but a few days later when her mother called her from the kitchen, in her hurry to obey she caught her foot in one of the chair's legs which was sticking out and went flying. Unfortunately, she fell on the cat which was sleeping peacefully and the yowling disturbed her father who was also having a nap. However much she protested that she *had* been looking where she was going and the chair moved from its place to be in the way, it had no effect. She was not allowed to have custard for tea.

When Kate sat on the chair again, weeks later, she did so extremely carefully. She put a little cushion on the seat first, then sat right in the middle, very still, with her drawing that she was finishing in her lap. After a while, she thought it would be safe to carry on drawing if she only moved her hand and arm.

All was well until she dropped her pencil and slowly leaned down to pick it up. There was an ominous crack as the left side leg of the chair snapped and flung her to the floor. She knew that she had not fidgeted once and she knew she had felt that chair shift to the left by itself but it was no use to say so. The chair was taken away from her and, after being mended, had been placed permanently in her parents' bedroom out of reach.

Kate told this story to Jane, who listened attentively and without interruption.

"So you see, my dear, that chair was bad," Helen finished. "It didn't ever want to be sat upon and didn't want to be with me. I think that coat is possibly another bad thing, so you couldn't stop it hurting Ivor. It's not your fault and he will wake up when his head is mended, so eat and enjoy your wafers."

As they now contentedly munched their treat, Helen thought what a terrible power guilt was. It should never have to be dealt with by a small, innocent child.

"By the way, are you not going to school?" she asked Jane, who shook her head in answer because her mouth was full. "Well, that's a pity now. Ivor won't know what's been happening when he wakes up. Should you not go perhaps and then tell him all the things you've learned while he slept. He won't want to miss anything and I'm sure he can hear you."

When they got back to the room, they found Laura had come back and was talking quietly to Helen. Jane gave her mother the last wafer that she had been saving with instructions to eat it for Ivor, then she went to her brother and stroked his cheek with her fingers.

Kate went on leave for a week after that. When she returned, Helen told her that Jane was back at school and whispering much more to her brother. The two women exchanged a secret smile and Kate, unusually, allowed herself to be hugged.

* * *

– 15 –

Bernie the Books was expecting visitors. Not just guests for dinner and not just any old guests. These were special ones, special to him anyway and he was looking forward to their arrival.

His diminutive wife Miriam, small as he was large, was bustling about singing happily to herself. She loved having visitors and a chance to show off her cooking skills. She had finished sprucing up the spare bedroom and making up the bed. Now she was planning menus and preparing food. When he got tired of listening to the clattering of pots, Bernie went into the kitchen.

"They're going to be pretty jet-lagged you know, Mim. They may need a good sleep before being stuffed solid with your most irresistible delicacies," he said, lifting her hair and kissing the back of her neck.

"That's all right," she replied, beaming at him. "I'm just doing something light for tonight with chicken soup first."

Ah, yes, thought Bernie, chicken soup. Jewish penicillin, the cure for all ills from acne to jet lag. He knew she was happy looking after people and missed having the kids at home, so he said no more but returned to his armchair and crossword puzzle. Five minutes later, she popped her head round the door just as he worked out that three down was an anagram of a word in the clue.

"Anyway, chicken soup will be best for Nancy's digestion after a long flight in her condition," announced Miriam.

"Her condition? What's that?" asked a slightly bewildered Bernie.

"It's obvious, you old silly," replied his wife. "All they would say on the phone was that they had some news.

They've been married about four months now. Think about it. She's pregnant."

That idea had not occurred to Bernie. The news could be anything good because they had sounded fairly cheerful. But his Miriam was a T.J.M., a Traditional Jewish Mother and any young woman saying she had some news only meant one thing. Sometimes Bernie was quite glad that their own two children were both sons.

"It could be anything," he said. "You're letting your imagination run riot. Perhaps they've won another pile of money on some sort of Australian game show."

"Pooh! Now who's got an overactive imagination?" retorted Miriam and went back into the kitchen.

The ones under discussion were Luke and Nancy. Nancy had telephoned Ziggy to say that they would be staying on with her parents for another four weeks in order to meet some people. Ziggy told her that Dr Evans had asked to extend his tenancy of the house for another month, so that fitted in nicely. If the dates didn't quite coincide, perhaps they could stay in a hotel for a few days.

All this was relayed to Bernie and Miriam and the T.J.M.'s reaction was typical as well as traditional. Their two boys had gone away to Europe for a gap year, whatever that meant, and the house was large and half empty as a result.

"They wouldn't be comfortable in a hotel and it costs too much," said Miriam, totally disregarding the fact that they had plenty of money and could probably afford The Ritz. "They must stay with us. It's far too quiet around here. It echoes and cooking for two all the time is boring. All you ever want is a steak."

There was really no answer to that but Bernie said, "OK, OK, already," because he loved her not only for her cooking.

Miriam's idea of something light for tonight was actually becoming a celebration welcome home dinner for eight people. Ziggy and his wife were invited of course and

Gerry would be bringing Luke and Nancy from the airport and then returning later with Dinah.

"Are you sure you're not doing too much food?" asked Bernie, wandering into the kitchen again.

He knew he could smell salt beef simmering in the pan without lifting the lid. He pinched one of the green beans Miriam was slicing and crunched contentedly on it.

"Anyone who wants to can always stop after the chicken soup," she replied calmly. "I haven't put any dumplings in it either."

"Thank goodness for that," murmured her loving husband and stole another bean.

At about half past five when Miriam had just put the kettle on, a cheery toot-toot was heard from the driveway and there was Gerry's car. He and two very suntanned young people scrambled out, grinning like chimpanzees.

"My but it's good to see you again," said Bernie, giving a hand each to Nancy and Luke while Gerry took an opportunity to kiss Miriam, with whom he always flirted shamelessly.

"Likewise," said Luke. "It feels as if we've been gone years instead of a few months. Even the grass looks a different colour."

Someone unloaded two small bags from the back seat and two big ones from the boot and Miriam said there was time for a cuppa before Gerry went to collect Dinah. She managed a surreptitious peek at Nancy's waistline but it was much too soon to detect any change. It was a thoroughly happy reunion. Soon Gerry excused himself to go home to the mews and change out of his chauffeur's clothes to bring Dinah.

"We're having a little welcome dinner party for you later," explained Bernie. "Only family or as near as dammit."

"Oh, wonderful," exclaimed Nancy. "I tried to get Dinah on the phone but she was never there."

Gerry looked slightly uncomfortable and muttered that he had better get going. When he returned an hour later, Ziggy and Nina, his wife, had arrived and there was a delicious savoury aroma in the house. Gerry produced a magnum of champagne from behind his back.

"This is for a special celebration toast before dinner," he announced, "as there seem to be most of the people I really care about under one roof."

Bernie rapidly produced eight glasses from a cabinet and yelled for Miriam to come from the kitchen. Nancy noticed that Dinah had turned bright pink and was fiddling with something in her handbag. She smiled to herself, as a question she had not yet asked had just been answered.

Gerry poured the champagne, not losing a drop, with the air of someone who did this every day. He proposed a toast to 'our gadabout youngsters, present and absent' so as to include Bernie and Miriam's sons. Then Bernie proposed another to the cook, hint hint. That cook, after draining her glass, ushered everyone to the dining table and lit the candles.

*

Nancy finished her bowl of soup with such relish that Miriam asked her if she would like a refill.

"I'd better not," she answered. "I think I can smell my favourite saltbeef so I must leave plenty of room."

She literally salivated as Bernie carved the succulent beef slices and nodded vigorously when he inquiringly held up a piece of the juicy golden fat. The contents of her plate were slowly but completely demolished. Nina caught Miriam's eye and they exchanged an unobtrusive nod. They both remembered what eating for two was like.

Finally a magnificent chocolate torte was delivered to the table, leaving everyone wondering if they still had a corner left inside to accommodate a taste. When the coffee pot was put down Bernie, who had been watching his wife and Nina watching Nancy, decided to take the bull by the horns, as it were.

"Luke, you said something about having some news when you telephoned. Am I right?"

"Yes, quite right," replied Luke. "Now that we're gathered together I see no reason for Nancy's parents to know more than you do any longer but I needed definite confirmation before we left Australia."

He paused for a gulp of coffee and a deep breath while all the others held theirs and looked at Nancy, who was serenely spooning cream into her cup.

"I've been offered a rather important job in Sydney and I've accepted," said Luke rather quickly, aware of a certain air of expectancy in the room. "The initial contract is for three years and begins in two months."

There followed complete silence. They were all still looking at Nancy, who was looking at her husband with unmistakable pride.

"The job is one close to my heart and something I've always had a deep interest in since schooldays," Luke went on. "I will be in charge of a huge research project into Down's Syndrome, sometimes called Mongolism. The salary is pretty good, too."

"But what about Nancy?" asked Miriam, suddenly recovering her wits.

"Oh, I think it's wonderful," said Nancy, "and my parents are there, of course. There's a very nice house thrown in and I love Sydney. Can't you just see me on Bondi Beach in my bikini?"

"There's a lot of sorting out to be done here, of course, one way or another," said Luke. I know it's a bit of a bombshell but we really do need your help."

"Of course, of course," said Ziggy. "Congratulations. In this day of modern technology, Australia isn't nearly as far away as it used to be. Anyway, you're not being transported for stealing a loaf of bread or something. You're being given a dream come true."

As if someone had pressed a button, they all started to chatter like magpies. Gerald enveloped his son in a great bear hug and his hand was shaken until he thought it would fall off. Then Bernie produced a bottle of vintage port and started another set of toasts.

"You're not driving home with all this booze inside you," Luke said to his father, laughing.

"No. We got a taxi here in anticipation and he's coming to take us back at 11.30, replied Gerald. "Zig and Nina are well within staggering distance."

Nancy's wits were still sharp. She noticed Gerald's use of 'we' and 'us' and the body language between him and Dinah. A lot can happen in four months and it looked to her as if it had. As they said their goodnights and see you tomorrows, she felt truly happy and not just for herself.

She helped Miriam to take the glasses into the kitchen, singing "I'm Sadie, Sadie, married lady," and giggling a little.

"I think I've had a bit to drink," she said confidingly.

"And so have I," replied Miriam. "D'you know, we thought your news was something quite different."

"Oh? What?" Nancy blinked at her.

"Well, it seemed a possibility, Sadie, married lady," and she patted Nancy's stomach gently.

Nancy stared for a moment, then burst out laughing.

"Oh, no. It's a bit soon. We'd like to get settled first but later on, definitely yes. And he or she will have the best of all extended families any baby could have all over the world."

The two women embraced, dancing round the kitchen, until Bernie put his head round the door.

"Time for bed," he said. "The fairies can finish the washing up while we sleep if I leave them that tiny drop of port in the bottle."

* * *

– 16 –

Dinah was feeling terrible. She didn't know what the hell was going on, for one thing. During the months after Nancy's wedding, Gerry had grown closer and closer to her. She found herself staying at the mews for the odd night after they had been to a late show sometimes, then for a whole weekend, ostensibly to taste some special wines. Then two or three days became a week and it seemed common sense for her make-up to find its place in an empty drawer.

All this time Dinah was slowly falling in love, much more dangerous than sudden infatuation. How could she have been such a fool, she thought? Fifty-eight years old and should know better, she ranted in her mind, while all she could really think about was his kindness when she was tired after work, his quirky sense of humour when she was down in the dumps and the fact that, after sixty-six years, Gerry had the mind of a healthy thirty-five year old and an untiring appetite for life.

Dinah had known nothing about Nancy and Luke coming back till the last moment or that she had been invited to the welcome dinner alongside Gerry. He had refused to go alone once he had collected his son and daughter-in-law from the airport, so Dinah had dressed rather hurriedly when he came back for her and felt less than her best when they arrived at Bernie's party. She felt a little bit better after the delicious meal and Gerry's attentions seemed to be concentrated on her and their relationship rather than drinking and joking with his son and their mates. But she just could not shake off the feeling that he was cooling off, that their affair was becoming one-sided.

Two days later, she got dressed for work to the accompaniment of Gerry munching on brown toast covered in peanut butter.

"I must go. I'm late," she said. "See you later."

"Yep. I'll be back by teatime," he replied, dropping a buttery kiss on her nose.

Dinah left feeling oddly empty, as if something was missing.

He hadn't even said where he was going. She felt like that all day long and plodded back to the mews with a heavy heart. The little car was parked outside, so at least Gerry had arrived home from wherever before her.

"Hello, love. Cuppa?" he asked, waving the teapot.

"Please," she replied kicking her shoes off.

"I'm glad you came home early. There's something I need to talk to you about," said Gerry.

Oh, here it comes. I knew it, thought Dinah. She said nothing but steeled herself against the worst, determined not to show her feelings.

"Luke and Nancy are going to be back for at least a month," Gerry went on. "I know Bernie and Nina are happy to have them but Luke does actually own this place, you know. I was wondering if I could come and stay with you and let them come and stay here."

"D'you mean to live?" asked Dinah, who had been holding her breath without realising it.

"Well, yes. Nothing would have to be moved because everything is still here, as it were. And it would only be for a few weeks while they sort the house out. What d'you think? Could you put up with me littering your fashionable flat?"

"Yes, of course," said Dinah. "It sounds a very sensible idea," and promptly burst into tears.

Gerry was up in a second, spilling tea all over the place and wrapping his arms round her.

"My dear girl, what is it? What's the matter? You don't have to do anything you don't want to. If it's that bad an idea, just forget I said anything."

"It's not that," she hiccuped. "I thought you were going to tell me you didn't want me any more."

"Oh, don't be daft, girl," he said, hugging her tightly. "Of course I want you. Can hardly remember what it was like before I had you except that it wasn't so good. I'm just a bit concerned about my globe-trotting son and your mate, Nancy. Bernie and Zig are good friends, personal as well as professional, but I'd rather give Luke back his own little pad while he's in England."

"Of course you would and so you shall," said Dinah, suddenly dry-eyed and strong once more, because she loved it when he called her 'girl'. "Can't we ring up now and tell him?"

No sooner said than done. Luke liked the idea but said it would have to be late the next day when they packed their bags again and took up residence in the mews. Gerry said that was fine and he'd change the bedclothes in the morning so there would be nothing for them to do but unpack. Then he and Dinah went to the Fruits de Mer for dinner. When they got back, they spent quite a lot of time seeing to it that the bedclothes were well and truly rumpled, definitely in need of changing.

Luke had put off moving accommodation because he had an appointment to visit the hospital early in the morning. As his last employment had been with them, certain information was needed by the authorities in Australia. Forms had to be signed and what amounted to testimonials given as to his character. Had he not been keen to visit and see his old workmates again, it might have become a bore but as it was, he looked forward to it.

The first thing Luke wanted to do was to find Dr Evans. Ziggy had seemed a bit vague about the reason for the extension to the rental of the house but said something about one of the children having an accident. He was greeted with enthusiasm by several people the moment he stepped through the hospital doors and was told that Dr Evans could be found, sooner or later, in the vicinity of children's I.C.U. On his way there, he heard hurried footsteps, then a familiar voice.

"Doctor, Doctor Benson, is it yourself, to be sure?"

"It was when I woke up this morning, my lovely shamrock blossom. I've missed you," he replied, as he turned and rather unprofessionally wrapped Sister Kate Malone in such a hug that her feet almost left the ground and her cheeks went quite rosy.

"Oh, behave yourself. You're a married man now. Have you the time for a quick cup of tea?" asked Kate, smoothing her skirt and setting an imaginary tilt in her cap straight.

"Of course and you can tell me where Dr Evans might be," said Luke.

"I'll do better than that. I'll take you to him," she replied, her voice suddenly serious, "but first a drop of tea," and she took his arm, leading him to her private sitting room.

Over tea they talked like the firm friends that they were, despite the age difference. Kate wanted to know all about his time in Australia and Luke told her of the magic second wedding ceremony and his new job offer. She loved to hear about dreams coming true for other people, as deep within her body there beat a romantic and ungrudging heart which was capable of sharing genuinely in the joy of others.

"Have you got to know my replacement?" Luke asked her and saw her smile fade and her eyes darken.

"Very well, only for the worst reasons," she replied sadly. "His little son lies here out of this world and the poor man's skills can do nothing to bring him back."

"I heard rumours of an accident," said Luke, shocked and misinterpreting the poetry of her Irish soul. "Is he alive?"

"Oh, he breathes sure enough, the only thing he does for himself. He's been deeply unconscious for about seven weeks now and the machines do all the rest for him, poor little mite."

"What happened? Do you know any details?" asked Luke.

"I think I may know more than Dr Evans or his wife, for the little girl has talked to me of things she perhaps wouldn't tell her parents. But I can tell you it happened when they were at play in the house and Ivor fell and banged his head on the stair post. There was nothing to see except a bruise and no fracture showed on the X-rays. He just hasn't woken up."

"Hm. D'you suppose I could see the boy? And Dr Evans if he's around?"

"Yes, he's probably there with him if we go now," said Kate, glancing at her watch and standing up. "Have you not met him yet?"

"No," replied Luke. "They rented our house but it was all done through the solicitors."

"Well, we must remedy that. They need all the friends they can get just now. Come with me," said Kate briskly.

*

What struck Luke about the children's intensive care unit was the quietness. Even when they opened the door to the room Ivor was in, the only sounds were the faint clicks and almost imperceptible hum of the machinery. A man with a shock of dark hair on his forehead was leaning over the bed adjusting something on a drip. He looked up with a question in his eyes.

"This is Dr Benson, Dr Evans," said Kate. "I've been just telling him about Ivor."

"The Dr Benson, in whose shoes I stand? The one who is married to my landlady?" he asked, sticking out his hand. "Gareth Evans. Pleased to meet you, only I wish it didn't have to be here."

"My heartfelt sympathy, Dr Evans. How is the boy?" replied Luke, liking the firm grip of his successor.

"Gareth. Call me Gareth. I'm just a man in this room. He's still sleeping."

Kate stood back, watching and sensing a bond forming as the two doctors bent over the child, murmuring softly and looking at dials on the machinery. She sat down, knowing that she would remain on watch for at least the next hour and busied herself with writing up some notes. This room was the one she called the 'lucky' room. Every child who had been in it had finally recovered with no exceptions. Kate began to think of them, trying to remember their names but it was no use. Her mind kept straying back to the little boy in the bed, silent and adrift in his own world where nobody could reach him. Suddenly, she realised that the doctors had moved to the door.

"Just off for a short break. See you later, Sister," said Gareth and he and Luke left together.

"I wish there was something I could do," said Luke. "As it happened in our house, I somehow feel responsible and I'm sure my wife, Nancy, would feel the same."

"Please don't worry," responded Gareth. "I know we asked for an extension but we'll actually be leaving in another week. We'll be going back to Wales."

"And your son? What about him?" asked Luke.

"I've been offered another job, one I applied for many months ago. It's at the big hospital in Swansea and comes with a house. They will take Ivor into their I.C.U. and send a life-support vehicle to transport him. Maybe a miracle will happen if we go back home."

"Maybe. Oh, I hope so, I really do," said Luke, grasping Gareth's hand. "I'll see to it that my solicitors arrange a rebate on your rent. Please keep in touch and let me know. Good Luck."

Impulsively the two men came together in a brief, wordless hug and then Luke turned away towards the administration office to tie up the ends of paperwork for his own future in a new job and a new country.

* * *

− 17 −

It felt extremely odd to be back in the old home. After all it was where they had spent their time living together and where they had consummated their marriage. So why, they wondered, did they feel that they had just stepped in from the mews and found themselves in somebody else's house? Admittedly, when Nancy went to the crockery cupboard for two mugs for their first coffee, declined by Gerry who was in a hurry to get to Dinah's flat, finding it full of food packets instead of china was no help. Nor was finding the food cupboard stacked with clean tea towels and a variety of paper rolls.

Luke, a touch fastidious about personal things, opened the bathroom cabinet to install his shaving gel and set off a noisy avalanche of containers, most of them empty.

"What untidy bugger made this unsavoury mess?" he roared.

"Your father," returned Nancy calmly. "Dinah doesn't shave."

Sheepishly, Luke returned his things to the toilet bag and left it open on top of the laundry box. Luckily, he didn't look inside and three days later, Nancy found the rumpled bedclothes and put them in the washing machine without saying anything.

Apart from making lists of things they had to do, there was little they actually could do until the house was vacated by the Evans family. So, feeling father naughty and idle, Luke and Nancy continued their honeymoon by going to London to see a couple of West End shows and do some shopping. The week sped by and Ziggy rang them at last to tell them they could pick up the keys.

Opening the door and stepping over the threshold of Roger's old house felt just as unreal to Nancy as it had the first time, when he had died. She knew she was being silly. For one thing, nobody she loved was dead and for another, she was now Mrs Luke Benson and not alone any more. Nevertheless, she was glad to hear her husband closing the front door decisively behind her.

"Don't you dare go and sit on those stairs. We've got work to do," he murmured into her ear, bringing the giggles bubbling up inside her.

"I suppose we'd better check the inventory," she said, when she could speak coherently.

The house had been left spic and span. Even the kitchen was clean and tidy. Nancy had given instructions for the tenants to put anything they didn't want to use or that got in the way up into the loft. She and Luke wandered from room to room but could see nothing missing or even out of place. Only one small item left them a bit mystified. On one of the beds upstairs, they found a small golden crown made of cardboard. Nancy tried it on but it was too small.

"Perhaps they had a fancy dress party or went to one," Nancy wondered out loud.

"Or maybe they gave hospitality to a dodgy princess. Have a look under the mattress and see if you can find a pea," said Luke, provoking yet another fit of the giggles.

"We'll have to decide what we want to take to Australia and we haven't discussed whether to re-let or sell the property," said Nancy, turning practical and producing a notebook and pen.

Luke had noticed milk in the fridge, tea bags in the cupboard and a tin with a note on top on the kitchen table. He had a peek in the tin and found it was, in fact, full of Welshcakes. Even in the midst of worry and grief, Mrs. Evans was a kind woman.

"Tea first," Luke said to his wife, "then work."

As it turned out, there seemed to be very little they wanted from the house or would even need in Australia.

The tiny antique oak bureau in which Aunt Miriam had kept her private bits and pieces was something which Nancy had always admired and perhaps even coveted. There were several paintings and Roger's fashion drawings, safely stored in a special chest, were also a must.

Bernie came up with the advice that, provided there was no special sentimental attachment, it might be better to sell the house rather than rent again. The investment market was very strong and they could always buy another house if they came back to live in England. Nancy agreed and Luke suggested they might like to buy a property in Australia in the meantime. Ziggy recommended a suitable estate agent and arrangements were made to put the house on the market.

Nancy had begun to realise that she was missing her parents quite a lot and wanted to get back to them as soon as possible. Shipping was arranged for the goods they wanted to take with them and she wondered if Gerry and Dinah would like anything from the house contents that were left. Gerry said he didn't want to be lumbered with any more possessions but Dinah asked if she could spend part of her day off helping Nancy with the sorting and look things over. Luke thought it would be a good idea for him to have a rest from making lists and go off with his father for a few rounds of golf.

*

When she opened the door, it occurred to Nancy that her friend and previous workmate was looking younger, slimmer and somehow much happier these days.

"I'm so glad you rang me," said Dinah. "I do need a few bits and pieces like extra bed linen, cushions and maybe kitchenalia for the flat. Also, I've been wanting to have a girls' session on my own with you and ask some advice."

"Well, let's have a cup of coffee first then," said Nancy, a little mystified and giving her friend a hug. "There's no hurry."

She wondered if this had anything to do with Gerry. Dinah had never talked much about her past or personal life and there was an age gap between them, although that never seemed to be a problem. So on went the kettle, out came the biscuit tin and they settled down companionably at the kitchen table. Dinah poured milk into her coffee and took a few appreciative sips.

"Tell me to shut up if I'm being personal," she said, "but what do you really think of your father-in-law?"

"I may not be the right person to ask, being a bit biased," chuckled Nancy, "I love him to pieces because he is so like Luke, only older. Things are getting serious with you two, aren't they?

"Yes," agreed Dinah, quietly. "Half of me feels like a horny teenager in the first grip of romance and the other half is just terrified and wants to run."

"I know you got divorced a couple of years ago but you've never said much about your husband. Did you have a bad time?"

It was as if that question opened the floodgates on a teeming river of pain, disappointment and anxiety. Dinah told of the dashing, charismatic marine engineer, six years her junior, who swept her off her feet. Oliver. He had a job high in the ranks of a large oil company and travelled the world, taking his new wife to exotic places with pride.

Then came the strange phone calls, coincidences, lost keys or wallets and mix-ups over names and places. There were references to Oliver's 'older sister, Dinah', for whom he had booked a room at a top hotel in New York to await his arrival. He had already arrived and was in the penthouse, in bed with the hotel owner's daughter. So it went on, woman after woman, lie after lie, tears following every new promise. Until, after 18 years of fake love and marriage, Oliver set his sights on the heiress of another oil company young enough to be his daughter and asked for a divorce. There were no children. He had sneaked off to have a vasectomy in Singapore.

"He gave me congenital herpes. Gerry doesn't know," Dinah finished, her hand shaking and her voice trembling with unshed tears.

Without a word, Nancy came round the table, put her arms around the older woman and held her tight for several minutes.

"You must tell him," she said finally. "Knowing Gerry, he'll probably say that you're lucky herpes is all the rotten bugger gave you."

"Honestly? You really think so?"

"Yes I do and that's the opinion of a happily married lady of five or so months' experience. And I reckon I'm going to have a kind, generous and lovely step mum-in-law before too long. Now what about these extras you need for the flat?"

*

The week after Dinah's visit, several people were sent to view the house with a surprising result. A Mr Roland Oakes made an offer of the full asking price with a rather unusual condition. He wanted the furniture included. It turned out that he had been living in fully-furnished property in Cyprus with his family for the past five years.

"Shall we accept?" Nancy asked Luke, when the agent rang with the news.

"Why not?" said Luke, slightly taken aback at the sudden speed with which their lives were moving. "Provided Ziggy thinks it's all right."

"Why not indeed," said Nancy, as it was raining and she was longing for the sunshine again.

The furniture they were taking to Australia was already on its slow sea journey but they had enough sense not to buy their plane tickets until the sale was nearing completion.

"Just as I was getting used to having you around again," grumbled Gerry, when his son began to seriously pack his suitcases, "and my gorgeous daughter-in-law."

"Don't whinge. You can come and visit, you know. We're not going to another planet," Luke retorted.

*

Things began to happen really fast after that. Then suddenly there they were, all standing on the doorstep of the mews, Luke and Nancy with bag and baggage, waiting for the taxi to come. They had refused all offers of a lift and what Gerry called a proper send-off.

"I suppose I've got to find clean bedclothes and make the bed," muttered Gerry.

"Well, we haven't had time," said Nancy, tongue in cheek. "We're family anyway, crazy though we may be and we're not dirty. So why change them at all? You don't mind, do you, Dinah?"

"I'd actually quite like to be part of this lovely, crazy family," said Dinah quietly.

Gerry looked at her sharply and she smiled at him, eyes full of love.

"Well that could be arranged without too much difficulty," Gerry said and took her hand.

When the taxi arrived, the luggage loaded, last hugs were distributed and Luke and Nancy were gone. Hand in hand, Gerry and Dinah turned and went indoors.

* * *

− 18 −

A tinny, irregular sound of drumming that went on and on and on was filling the house. When Patricia could stand it no longer, she went to the foot of the stairs, gathered her breath, held on to the bannisters and yelled with all her strength.

"Quentin. Quentin, will you shut UP! Come down, it's tea time."

She went back into the kitchen to finish slicing the bread for sandwiches. Glancing out of the window, she saw her husband making his way up the path, a rake propped on his shoulder like a soldier with a rifle. She smiled to herself. It was good to have a bit of garden, especially at the back of a town house and big enough for a vegetable patch as well as flowers. There was a small plum tree as well, that looked as if it might flourish and fruit next season. Plum and almond tart was one of Patricia's special puddings. The downside to that was wasps, of course, always on the lookout for ripe plums.

They'd had no garden when they lived in Limassol, except the seashore. Roly used to say it didn't matter. because their crop was wild oysters and clams and everyone else grew vegetables in great abundance. Mother Mediterranean was generous and the harvest almost continuous in the mild climate of Cyprus. The Oakapple, which was the name of their tiny restaurant, was successful. It certainly made plenty of money, enough for them to afford a top school for their son. The kind of school one could only find in England, according to Roly.

This was one of the main reasons why they had sold up and come home, two months before Quentin's twelfth birthday. He was not their fifth child as his name might suggest but he was the fifth male to be born into the Oakes family in the past century. As far as they could trace, that is. Before his father was born, there had been a long line-up of females. Quentin was a bright boy, outstripping the others at the happy-go-lucky junior school in Limassol and disappearing after lessons onto the beach to play, not football but first his recorder and then a clarinet. Now, back in England and in a new house, it was drums as well.

Roland Oakes was a big man. He was broad without being fat and had to bend his head to get in the back door.

"Boots, please," said his wife mildly when she heard him enter, sending him back to grunt as he pulled off the offending muddy footwear.

"Has he come down yet?" he asked. "I heard you shouting, as did the whole street I should think."

She shook her head and he padded out to the foot of the stairs in his socks.

"QUENT!" he bellowed. "Get yourself down here."

This had an effect, of sorts. With a sound that could only be described as a train whistle in need of repair, his son came hurtling down, lying across the polished pine bannister rail on his stomach. He landed on his feet and enveloped his father in a bear hug from shoulder to knee.

"No need to shout, Dad," said Quentin as he released his hold.

Quentin Oakes was tall at twelve years old, coming up to just below his father's chin. That height included the thick shock of straw-coloured hair which trailed on his forehead. Not as brawny yet as Roland, his hands were long and slender and his feet matched them. Although his parents considered him a trifle undisciplined, he was a happy boy with a quick mind. His mother had always been secretly enchanted by him but tried hard not to show it.

"Tomato sandwiches and scones to keep you going until dinner time," she announced, pouring tea into sensible sized mugs. "I've got a list from the internet of the schools prepared to take on new pupils," she went on. "Don't know if you'll have any preferences but you'd better take a look at it."

Quentin gave a little groan but pulled the sheet of paper towards him, leaving it between himself and his father so that they could both see it. The only sound for a few minutes was the slow munching of crusty bread.

"There's one here," said Roly eventually in a slightly muffled voice. "Got a rather odd name. Cholmonderley and Cecil. Moderate success academically but their speciality is music."

"Where? Let me see. Show me," said Quentin, waking up and showering the table with crumbs.

"Thought that might get your attention," said his father. "The drawback is that you might have to board there because it's quite a distance over to the East from here."

"Not that it would matter," Patricia joined in. "Term times are short these days and holidays are long. Mind you, the cooking won't be nearly as good as home."

"Right then," said Roly, sitting back and taking a scone. "We can send off for the paperwork on that one first. Cholmonderley and Cecil."

"I think you'll find that it's pronounced 'Chumly'. Most of the aristocrats who kick off with these names seem to suffer from lazy speech, even if they don't drop their aitches," said Patricia dryly. "Worth remembering if you ever speak to any of them."

There was no need to bother with the other schools on the list. In an amazingly short time, they received an invitation to visit the school. They went away for two days, staying at a good hotel nearby. Quentin took to the headmaster, who apparently played the cornet extremely well, and was permitted to try the piano in one of the spacious studios. The fees were affordable to the Oakes and the outcome was sealed by the information that the famous Chuck Fineberg, one of Quentin's idols, had graduated from the very halls of the C. and C. Quentin was to start the following term.

They had to go to London, of course, to have uniforms etc. measured for and fitted. This meant another few days away in a good hotel. By the time they went shopping for the largest tuck box they could find, the whole thing had taken on the air of a holiday trip. Then came the day when Quentin, unperturbed, waved his parents goodbye from the gates on the first day of his first term at the school which he would one day leave to become a famous musician.

"I miss my kitchen," announced Roly, when they were having lunch on Patricia's birthday at the Fruits de Mer. "I wonder if they could use a sous chef here, perhaps on busy weekends."

"Why not ask? I'm missing Quentin a bit actually, so you could ask them if they need a head waitress at the same time," said Patricia sharply, annoyed that he couldn't think of better things to say on her day of the year.

Roly did ask, however, at the Fruits de Mer, and it was suggested that he come to see Francois on the following morning before the lunch hour.

*

"Fridays, Saturdays and whenever an emergency arises, on a month's trial. Sort of loose and freelance," Roly explained to his wife when he returned from the interview, rather elated. "They've got plenty of spare waitresses though, my Patsy."

"Doesn't matter," she replied. "I daresay I'll think of something. In fact, I've already had one idea, although it's as much for you as it is for me."

"Oh, yes? Go on," said Roly, beginning to look a little wary.

"Well, we haven't properly explored the loft in this house yet and at first glance it appeared to be spacious but full of clutter."

"Ye-es," said Roly, head on one side and even more wary.

"The way this house is built, the flooring should be pretty solid and it may be at least partly soundproof," his wife went on. "I was thinking that it might make a good studio for Quentin if he stays interested in music. Could even double up as a bedroom and give him privacy. After all, he's almost a teenager."

Roly relaxed, relieved that it was nothing more threatening than nest shuffling.

"And we are almost middle-aged fogies. That's what you were thinking, I know," he said. "But it's an idea worth expanding. I suppose I could start by clearing the clutter out."

Roly was as good as his word. For the next two days, the house resounded with thumps, clatters and rattles until Patricia was almost expecting a sharp rap on the front door from a disturbed and irate neighbour. Cardboard boxes slid down the loft ladder and arrived on the landing, sometimes spilling out their contents. When Patricia went to investigate, she found herself suddenly enveloped in a thick, pink, old-fashioned eiderdown. She stood there for a few minutes, looking like an enormous pink marshmallow with feet, until Roly lifted up the end and poked his head in to grin at her.

"It's like Aladdin's cave up there," he said. "Come up and help me."

"OK, if you'll help me clear up this mess down here," she replied. "And don't start rubbing any lamps you may find."

"Of course. Allow me to assist you onto the stairway to discovery," said Roly, putting both hands round her neat buttocks and gently heaving her up the ladder.

She decided, once she got there, that Aladdin's cave was not a bad description, although a lot of it would probably only be fit for the local jumble. She did, however, find a box which was full of old recipe books and magazines and would definitely be most useful in the future. Another box revealed dozens of intriguing fashion drawings.

"Come and look at what I've got here," Roly said suddenly.

He was squatting in front of a large wicker hamper, fiddling with something in a heavy zipped-up bag. He got the zip undone and wrinkled his nose at the unmistakable smell of moth balls. Plunging an enquiring hand inside the bag, he pulled out a sleeve with a velvet cuff. It felt wonderfully soft.

"Let's get this one down for a closer look, Patsy," he said, dragging the hamper to the top of the ladder.

"These books too, please," replied his wife, glad of the chance to get down into the house and pushed her box over to him.

It took some amount of heaving and shoving but they finally lowered their burdens down the ladder without damaging anything or even breaking a fingernail.

"Coffee first, then an examination," said Patsy firmly and marched downstairs into the kitchen with the box of cookery books in her arms.

*

Later, Roly retrieved the zipped-up bag from the hamper. He laid it flat on the sofa, unzipped it completely and carefully withdrew the contents. His first thought was that it looked very expensive. Running his hands gently over the velvet collar confirmed this impression, as did the strange and attractive horn button at the top. He searched in vain for some kind of label and gave up. Patricia was busily leafing through a recipe magazine.

"This is a coat, my Patsy," said Roly, "and if I'm not entirely mistaken, it is no ordinary coat."

"What is?" murmured his wife, who was beguiled by a quite extraordinary recipe for something called flummery.

"The mystery of the zipped-up bag. It's a lady's overcoat and it looks unworn and extremely pricey. Try it on."

To please him, she stood up and held out her arms. The garment slid on easily and settled as if it were used to being there. Patsy's hand roamed over the collar to the big horn button and lingered there, fingers caressing the smoothness. She gave a little twirl.

"You look lovely," said Roly, catching his breath slightly. "It's yours. You must have it. It's as if it were made for you."

"No," she replied, with a hardness in her voice he had never heard before. "I can't wear this," and she shrugged out of the coat, dropping it back into the hamper.

"Why ever not?" asked Roly, mystified. "It suits you. Matches your eyes."

"Yes, it's green and I don't wear green. It's extremely unlucky for certain people, didn't you know? There's no way I'll ever wear it. Put it in the charity shop pile."

Next morning, the mountain of goods for the charity shop was waiting in the hall, the zipped-up bag with the coat in it on top.

"Can you get all that in the car?" asked Patricia.

"Yes, all except this," answered Roly, picking up the bag and putting it in the hall cupboard.

"What are you doing with it, then? I won't wear it and I don't even want it in the house," said Patricia with ill concealed anger.

"It's far too good for any charity shop," said Roly firmly. "I'm going to put it up for sale on eBay and see what happens."

* * *

– 19 –

Looking out at the early morning mist drifting down the valley, the old man thought how beautiful it all seemed. He stretched widely, taking in a great gulp of fresh air, then shut the bathroom window, replacing the net curtain neatly. The shrill whistle coming from the kettle encouraged him to pad downstairs into the kitchen. Una, his wife, was already buttering the toast.

"You were a long time, cariad," she greeted him. "I thought you'd decided to have a shower."

"No, no. I want to get going early today and it's past seven now," he replied.

"Are you going to choir practice first, then?" Una asked.

"Not today. I'm going straight to the hospital. You can still come with me if you want."

Stefen Thomas had been a member of the Treorchy Male Voice Choir for as long as he could remember. Although a little rusty, his voice was still good and clear enough to swell the numbers on special occasions. He rarely missed a practice but he had awoken on this particular morning with a feeling of urgency which he was unable to explain. For some unknown reason, he wanted to get to the hospital as quickly as possible, although he usually went to see his little grandson in the afternoon each day.

"No, you go without me. I've made an appointment to have my hair done this morning," said Una. "If I cancel I won't get another one for a few days. Give my love to everyone and I'll come with you tomorrow."

*

Treorchy had a long, straight main high street, full of shops on either side with two or three pubs and a town hall scattered in between. Stefen drove along it to the newsagents to pick up yet another packet of his favourite blackcurrant sweets. They helped him to concentrate when he was driving. He had never smoked in all his life, which could be the reason why his voice was still so good at 72 years old. He found a free parking right outside the shop.

"Bore da, good morning Mr Thomas. You're about bright and early. The usual, is it?" asked Sarah, the owner's wife, always seemingly on duty and unfailingly cheerful.

"Yes, please. It's a lovely day now the mists have gone," he replied, fishing a fifty pence piece from his pocket.

It had been suggested that it would be cheaper to buy these sweets in bulk but Stefen preferred the weekly contact. He had known Sarah and her husband for a long time, as he had most of the older folk in town.

"You'll be seeing the boy today no doubt. Has there been any change, poor little mite?" asked Sarah as she passed over the packet of sweets.

Stefen shook his head sadly, remembering how he always shared them with his grandson when he had the chance. He hurried back to the car, still feeling that he must get to the hospital early. Popping one of the blackcurrant drops into his mouth, he had to hold back from speeding down the High Street. He kept a steady pace below the limit on the road to Neath, in spite of the urge to put his foot down. Turning towards Swansea and the coast, he had to be patient in the last of the rush hour traffic but eventually he turned into the gates of the big hospital with a sigh of relief.

They had been very kind and given him special permission to park close to the intensive care unit. He had been every day ever since the boy arrived a month before and many people knew him. There were a few waves and greetings as he made his way in. He knew he would see his son-in-law before long, so he went straight to the room, this time with haste, giving way to this inexplicable need to hurry.

The room was empty of people, save for the occupant of the bed. Stefen could see that all the machinery was working as usual, the tubes and bottles in place and there seemed to be no change at all from the day before. The small, pale face, eyes closed in deep sleep, was still in the same place on the pillow.

"Ivor," said Stefen, gently touching the motionless little head. "Ivor, Grandad is here."

There was no response. He drew up the comfortable chair they had provided for him, settled close by the child avoiding all the paraphernalia and began to sing. The soft baritone, like a melodious whisper, seemed to bond with the hum and occasional click of the machinery. One after another he sang all the old familiar songs of Welsh childhood. The young nurse, who had gone for a quick toilet break, crept back into the room and resumed her vigil, silently checking the machines and dials. Then she sat down on her hard, straight-backed chair and listened. She let the voice wash over her mind, lulling and relaxing the tension and tiredness, bringing her own safe childhood back to her.

It had become Stefen's habit to watch his grandson's face the whole time, as if trying to imprint it onto his own brain to take with him when he left. He was half way through Men of Harlech when he thought he saw the child's eyelid flutter. His voice faltered a fraction and he looked more closely. No, he must have been mistaken. The small face was still as ever. Perhaps, he thought, he too would have a short break in a minute. He began the last verse, moving closer to the bed. Suddenly and without a shadow of doubt, both the boy's eyelids flickered. Stefen looked at the nurse and it was obvious that she had seen it as well. It was not just wishful thinking. Almost joyfully, the girl pressed the big red emergency button.

First through the door was Gareth Evans, followed by the staff nurse.

"Don't stop singing, please Dad," he said to Stefen and bent over his son.

The staff nurse was rapidly adjusting machinery, the young nurse was trying to explain what had happened, then as Men of Harlech took on a slightly triumphant tone, Ivor opened his eyes. Everyone except Stefen became very quiet. Stefen took his little grandson's hand, at least the part of it that was free of tubes and attachments, and went on singing. He fell silent when he saw the boy's lips part and a moment later a sound emerged.

"Graaanthaa," was what it sounded like and Stefen felt two small fingers tighten on his large one.

"I think he's trying to say Grandad," said Stefen in a very shaky voice.

Two more doctors turned up and requested that everyone leave the room except the boy's father. The two nurses and Stefen stepped into the corridor in a daze. The younger nurse gave Stefen a hug and kissed his cheek, probably risking her job but she did it anyway.

"It was your wonderful singing that did it," she said. "I have heard that people in a coma for a long time often come close to the surface and almost wake up. If nothing happens to help or encourage them, they drop back down again. Perhaps Ivor came up like that, heard you singing and it woke him. It's so exciting. Nothing like this has ever happened before when I've been on duty."

"Hush now, my girl, you're gabbling. Someone should get the boy's mother," said the staff nurse, losing her habitual stiffness and going away with a foolish grin playing round her mouth.

Stefen rang Una to tell her the news and say he would be home later, ignoring the rules about not using mobile phones. He felt he had certainly had enough choir practice for one day and of the best kind too. Then his daughter arrived with his granddaughter, who couldn't stop chattering with excitement and the little party outside the door swelled even more when the staff nurse returned, still unable to stop smiling.

Eventually the door opened and silence fell. Not a whisper. Gareth appeared first and he was smiling too as everyone gathered around him.

"He's fine" he announced, with a little choke in his voice. "Preliminaries show that there appears to be no lasting damage and he'll recover completely. But deeper tests need to be made and we'll have to build him up again now so he'll be here for a few more days. You can go in now for a little while but not too long, please. Remember we've got the rest of our lives now and so has he, so go easy."

Gareth's voice had begun to tremble and he put his arms round his wife and daughter. He understood now why it was not the done thing for doctors to treat their own loved ones. They all shuffled back into the room, staff nurse as well. The small face that greeted them open-eyed from the bed looked less wan and colour had crept back into his cheeks. Jane went immediately to her brother, clambered up on the bed and put her lips to his ear. The boy smiled.

Stefen looked round the room and nodded at his daughter. Then very softly he began to hum. Presently, the melody of an old song filled the room like a distant murmur as they all joined in. "There'll be a welcome in the hillside, when you come home again to Wales."

Afterwards, Helen Evans asked if everyone had been informed and was rewarded by cheerful affirmatives. Then Gareth said "Oh, no!" and punched his forehead with the heel of his hand.

"Who? Who doesn't know?" asked Helen, concerned that there might be someone who was still worrying.

"Kate," replied Gareth. "Sister Kate Malone back at the General. I promised her. I'll ring her now," and he hurried off.

When he returned, he looked a bit crestfallen and disappointed.

"Did you get her? What did she say?" asked Helen.

"She was off duty but I left a message. She'll get it. They won't let me down," said Gareth.

He put one arm round his wife and the other round Jane and hugged them close.

"We're lucky, we're so lucky. I love you all very much," he said.

*

Kate Malone hardly had time to take her coat off when she came back on duty at the General Hospital before someone said "Sister, there's an urgent message for you. It came this morning."

She wondered what on earth could be urgent in her life at the moment. However, she made her way at once to her office and was told again twice on the way by two other people. So it was with some trepidation that she picked up the folded slip of paper from her desk with her name on it in bold letters and read it.

'Ivor woke up 10.35 this morning. All is well. No damage. Our love and thanks. Dr Gareth Evans.'

The piece of paper fluttered to the floor as Kate made the sign of the cross with a shaking hand.

"Jesus, Mary and Joseph, you heard me and you granted my request. Thank you, thank you. May the family have a happy life now," she whispered.

Her tears of joy and relief fell soundlessly on the head of the small figurine of the Virgin which stood on Kate Malone's desk.

* * *

– 20 –

All along the high street in Minchester, the wooden tubs stood almost in waiting mode. They had been planted with winter pansies but only a few orange blooms showed their faces. Everyone knew, of course, that there were bulbs in between beneath the soil, perhaps daffodils or tulips and that they would make a blaze of colour later. Meanwhile, the effect was of dormancy and perhaps a little dull.

Elsie was feeling anything but dull as she made her way along the street, the heels of her new smart shoes tapping rhythmically on the pavement. In fact she barely noticed that there were tubs there at all. Not only were her shoes new but so was her coat and trilby type hat. The coat had two big pockets on each side, studded with gold buttons and a short stand-up collar. The whole effect was slightly military from a distance, a fact which had escaped Elsie's notice also. She just knew that the outfit made her feel great and fashion wise, younger than her years. Which was just as well since she was on her way to chair a fairly important meeting at the Chamber of Commerce.

First she needed to make sure that Veronique, alias Veronica, had arrived to open the shop. Elsie was pleased with Ronnie, as she was called by her family and when she was alone with Elsie. She had been taken on as head assistant six months previously because Elsie saw beneath the surface. Ronnie looked the part, for a start, dressing well for a girl of meagre means and moving like a model. Also she talked the correct talk without sounding false. In fact, there was a bit of the actress in her and she had proved herself to be honest and reliable. Checking on her was not really necessary, therefore. Elsie simply wanted to see the girl and say good morning, which had recently begun to include a peck on both cheeks, French style, but without the accompaniment of the popular 'moi, moi' sound. Ronnie was fast becoming a surrogate daughter to the childless Elsie.

"Good morning, Mrs Lehman. I hope you're well. Do love your outfit. It makes you look taller and somehow important," she trilled. "Are you going somewhere special?"

"Thank you, my dear. I tried to look the part as I've got to be chairlady this morning. There's lunch afterwards as well, so it's sandwiches behind the screen for you, I'm afraid. Did you remember to bring something?"

"Oh, yes. Please don't worry. They're only cheese and tomato so I won't make a smell. You go off and do your thing with those silly people. They can't do without you, you know."

"I suppose," said Elsie, bridling a little and adjusting her hat unnecessarily, "but I do worry about you. Perhaps one evening when you're not seeing your boyfriend, you'd like to come and have a nice dinner with me."

"That would be lovely, Mrs Lehman. Now don't worry and don't be late," replied Ronnie, edging her employer towards the door, and breathing a sigh of relief as she closed it after her.

Ronnie was grateful for her job and genuinely tried to please Elsie but she did get a bit much sometimes. Ronnie didn't actually have a boyfriend at the moment but invented one in order to avoid seeing Elsie out of working hours. Enough was enough. She trotted to the back of the shop to put the coffee on, one of the smells the customers, or clients as Elsie preferred to call them, seemed to like.

*

Elsie arrived at the Chamber's headquarters in good time and was greeted effusively.

"Elise, you're looking lovely today. Oh Elise, how are you, moi, moi? Elise, let me take your gorgeous coat. Is it a one-off or are you stocking it this season? Here's the info for the meeting, Elise, although I'm sure you, have it all in mind."

Nobody ever called her Elsie these days. It was only on her passport and private cheque or similar paraphernalia which did not apply to the shop. She rather liked it that way. It was vaguely exciting, like being a spy or a film star with a double life. She had become someone important, particularly at the Chamber and she never invited any of the members to call on her socially. That would spoil everything. It was better to remain slightly mysterious.

Somebody took Elsie's coat to hang up and she settled down in the comfortable Victorian leather chair behind the desk to look at the notes while everyone assembled. The subject for discussion and possible judgement was the local shoe shop. Established for 100 years in the same family, the present younger Mr Wentworth had a gripe about the local plant and gardening shop which had been in the High Street for a mere 30 years.

Mr Wentworth observed that for the last 6 months, the said gardening shop had begun to stock wellington boots, also rubber and plastic overshoes. The shoe shop had sold these items with the very best leather footwear for ladies and gentlemen, since the younger Mr Wentworth took charge. He did not welcome the new competition from what he decided were goods of lesser quality. What he would welcome was decisive interference by the Chamber to put a stop to it.

Elsie's sympathy actually lay with the gardening shop. She herself had begun to stock the odd hat in Elise. It began with only the odd one or two as window dressing but, to her surprise, she sold the first three she tried under her rule that everything put in the shop should be for sale if requested. She made a hefty profit too, as she bought the hats from the internet, described as 'unwanted gifts still in box' or 'worn once only'. To be on the safe side, she sprayed them with steriliser and odourless forms of insecticide. The only milliner in town was at the other end of the High Street and had probably never heard of Elise, but Elsie firmly believed that people in glass houses should not throw stones.

The meeting droned on for an hour or more before it was decided that rubber wellies were, in fact, gardening goods and even somewhat out of place in a shop which advertised fine footwear. Mr Wentworth consoled himself with two large glasses of Beaujolais over lunch at the Yew Tree while Elsie sipped an elegant Riesling. Then she drifted back to Elise, where Ronnie decided that they may as well change the small side window, as the velvet skirt displayed in it had just been sold.

Apart from the fact that she could trust her, Veronica proved to be very good for Elsie. There was a small computer in the shop, only used for business accounts, regular customers' particulars, details of trade fairs and suchlike. Ronnie, however, insisted on showing Elsie how to play with it, make it do things and use the internet. For one normally so set in her ways, Elsie was a quick learner and it was not long before she wanted to have one at home.

One Thursday afternoon, when things were always slack, she closed the shop and took Ronnie off to choose a suitable personal laptop. When the deed was done, Ronnie was treated to posh pricey afternoon tea at Perryloves, an out of London copy of Fortnum and Masons. Afterwards they spent an hour or two at Elsie's flat, practising laptopping and sipping sherry. It turned into a special occasion as Elsie realised that it was the first time she had invited anyone into her home since David's funeral.

Before too long, as Elsie played with her new toy every spare evening, she found eBay. At first, she was rather taken aback at the amount and variety of goods offered for sale and feared for the ultimate life span of normal shops and boutiques such as Elise. Then she saw the first hat and decided tentatively to join in the fun. The hat was obviously designer and fashioned from copper-coloured feathers. It exactly matched a suit which she had just put on display in the shop window.

Elsie bid for the hat, hesitantly at first but she got it for ten pounds although she would have been happy to pay more. She was half expecting rubbish but, on examination when it arrived, she decided it could only have been worn once if at all. To add to her conviction, she discovered a tiny 'Yasmine' label under the inside band. She and Ronnie laid it reverently on a small table by the suit in the window. The next day, a lady bought the suit and insisted she have the hat to go with it. Elsie pointed out the label and suggested an extra cost of seventy-five pounds.

"How very reasonable," said the lady, producing her credit card. I'm so glad I found you. I shall come again."

That was the beginning. Elsie was hooked on eBay and her comfy flat became a glass house.

On the evening after the Chamber of Commerce meeting, rubber wellies and shoes were still on Elsie's mind. She wondered if she should buy any more hats or if anyone would notice and make trouble. Nevertheless, the addiction was by now too strong and she switched on anyway but avoided hats. Everything else that evening seemed rather boring until she came to a coat, a green coat. She peered, fiddling to try to get a bigger picture and could hardly believe her eyes.

"That's my coat. MY coat," she said accusingly. "What are you doing with my coat?"

She looked more closely and there was no doubt. The velvet collar and cuffs and there was the button, the big horn button. There could never be another button the same as that one.

"Why are you trying to sell my coat?" Elsie asked the machine stupidly, wondering if she had drunk too much wine. "If you didn't want it, why take it from me in the first place?"

Because it was in the shop and everything in this shop should be for sale. That is the rule, a nasty, spiteful little voice in her mind answered. She realised that her hand was shaking. There was a reserve of fifty pounds on the coat and as she watched, a bid of fifty-five was made. A mixture of determination, disbelief and anger stopped Elsie shaking and, as if in a dream, she made a bid of sixty.

She waited and thought suddenly that she must not use her real name here. Nobody must find out that the owner of Elise was bidding for clothes on the internet. It would mean embarrassment at least and total ruin at worst. Particularly as she noticed that the address of the seller was local. Up came another bid of seventy and she decided to put a stop to this game if possible and worry about details later. After all, she could pay cash and collect, use her single name if necessary. She tapped in a bid of a hundred pounds. There was a long wait while she hoped it was enough to frighten the opposition. Time was ticking away and it finally ran out. 'You have been successful', she read and let out a long shuddery sigh.

Elsie had won her coat back. Now all she had to do was go to collect it and pay. She found the address was not far away but the one thing that worried her was meeting that awful bully of a man again with his poor, downtrodden mother. He had all but stolen her coat and she didn't even know his name, let alone his address. And why would he sell the coat for so little, having paid so much? There was only one way to find out, thought Elsie, and plucking up her courage, she sent off an e-mail.

* * *

– 21 –

"Get that will you, love," called Roland, as the doorbell gave its insistent buzz. "I expect it's the woman about the coat."

"Why can't you go? It was your idea," replied Patricia, but appeared out of the kitchen anyway just as Roly backed out of the big hall cupboard, bottom first.

"OK. We'll both go," he said, throwing an arm over his wife's shoulders.

Elsie was about to give the bell another short try when the front door flew wide open. She found herself confronted by a huge bear of a man with tousled hair, wearing only dungarees and socks. His arm was around a most attractive woman with blonde hair and wearing an apron. She knew she had never seen either of them in her life and began to feel less nervous.

"Er… I'm Elsie Young. I made the bid for the coat," she said hesitantly.

"Oh, yes. Do come in and have a good look at it," said Roly, releasing Patricia and standing back with a welcoming gesture.

Looking at the woman's dowdy grey raincoat and headscarf, he thought it was certainly about time she bought herself some decent clothes. As they went through the hall, Elsie caught a delicious aroma of baking. She couldn't help lifting her head and giving a little sniff, which did not go unnoticed.

"Would you like a cup of coffee?" asked Patricia.

"Thank you, that would be nice," replied Elsie, her fears of a confrontation diminishing with every second.

She was ushered into a sitting room overlooking a pleasant garden. A zipped-up clothing protector was draped over one of the armchairs and Roly picked it up.

"Do sit down," he said to Elsie, unzipping the cover and taking the coat out. "Here it is. Your coat."

Elsie almost fell into the chair and drew a sharp breath. It was indeed her coat. She recognised it at once and felt her face flush with pure joy of seeing it again.

"Yes, it is quite special, isn't it? I'm glad you feel it too," said Roly.

"It looks far better than the picture. I'm so glad I found it," said Elsie softly, reaching out to stroke a velvet cuff gently as if it were a puppy.

"Well, you'd better try it on," said Roly briskly, holding it out to her. "It looks as though it will fit you but you never know."

Elsie stood up and shrugged out of her mackintosh. She slipped her arms into the coat and it seemed to wrap itself around her like a lover. She caressed the horn button, enjoying the almost sensual feel of it.

"There you are. Perfect. Could have been made for you," said Roly, as Patricia came in with a laden tray.

"My feelings exactly. You look gorgeous," she said. How do you like your coffee?"

"Milky with no sugar, please," said Elsie, coming out of her reverie and taking the coat off.

"Have one of these tarts, too," said Patricia. "I've been trying out a new recipe."

"Is the coat yours?" asked Elsie, after taking a sip of coffee. "It looks as if it has never been worn."

"No, it's not mine," replied Patricia. "I don't wear green. It was in the attic along with a load of other stuff when we bought this house. It just seemed too good for a charity shop."

"What about the previous owners?" asked Elsie, still mystified.

"They were a young couple who emigrated to Australia. We never met them. It was all done through solicitors."

"That's lucky for me, then," said Elsie, opening her bag and putting two crisp new fifty pound notes on the coffee table. "And these tarts are delicious."

"Thank you," said Patricia. "A pile of old cookery books were hiding in the attic as well and some of the recipes are most unusual. Would you like to take the rest of these tarts home for later? I've made plenty."

"How kind. Thank you so much," murmured Elsie, her mind still fuzzy with disbelief at the way things were turning out.

Patricia took the plate away, vaguely wondering if this rather nondescript woman was all there in the head. A hundred pounds for a second-hand coat? Without knowing why, she felt a bit sorry for her and returned with a bag containing six tarts.

*

Elsie hurried home with her precious burden, resigned to not solving the mystery of how her coat found its way back to her. Really, she no longer cared. It was meant for her, her coat, and she would be going to Milan with an invitation to a fashion show. Just the occasion to wear her coat properly for the first time. It would have to be expertly cleaned to get rid of the smell of mothballs but she knew the best person for that. Elsie felt more than content. In a strange way she felt complete.

The following days passed in a flurry of activity for Elsie. She would be in Milan for four days and Ronnie had to be schooled to run the shop by herself. Elsie of late had been seriously thinking of making the girl her partner in the business, especially as she had no relatives of any closeness to inherit anything. She knew Ronnie was to be trusted as far as money was concerned, to keep honest accounts, pay into the bank and attend to security, which was important.

Accidents can happen and planes do crash. Elsie decided that the deed should be done before she went on her trip. She rang her solicitor, made an appointment for him to come to the flat and sat Ronnie down to explain her intentions. To say that Ronnie was open-mouthed with astonishment was no exaggeration. She thought at first that it was some strange type of joke but she was a kind girl and her tender heart flooded with compassion when she realised that her employer had plenty of wealth and position but nobody close to love or lean on when in difficulty. She agreed to the proposal but with certain unusual conditions because she, in turn, trusted Elsie.

"Please don't think I'm rude or ungrateful, Mrs Lehman, because of what I'm going to suggest," said Ronnie, her eyes on Elsie's face and her hands folded in her lap. "I have a mum and dad and I love them but sometimes it's too close, if you see what I mean. I've often wished that I had an auntie perhaps that I could talk to about things without her getting over protective. Could you maybe consider, quite unofficially of course, adopting me as a sort of niece as well as a business partner? As far as I'm concerned, it would mean I could do a lot more for you on a personal level, which is something I've really wanted to do for a while now. You've done so much for me and I'd like to give back as well as take. There. Now I've probably offended you and made you cross," she finished with a little sigh.

There was silence for a moment, as both women sat deep in thought. When Elsie spoke, it was with a slight catch in her voice.

"On the contrary, I'm extremely touched, my dear. I had an older sister once with whom I had that special relationship but she died. I would very much like to have you as a surrogate niece as well as a business partner," declared Elsie. "We needn't tell everybody about the niece bit, just keep it to ourselves. You could stop calling me Mrs Lehman when we're alone together, for a start. My sister used to call me Elly and that will do nicely. The solicitor's coming to the flat at ten tomorrow, so you come a bit earlier. We'll put everything into his hands and open the shop after lunch."

*

Ronnie must have made a good impression the next day on Elsie's usually dour solicitor because he was smiling long before he left. An equal partnership was arranged, the business to pass to the surviving partner on the demise of one of them. Elsie also made arrangements for a more substantial salary to be paid to Ronnie monthly and an annual share of the profits. The documents were promised to be ready for signature in three days.

Elsie made what she called a scratch lunch of tinned mushroom soup and smoked salmon sandwiches. Ronnie had never eaten smoked salmon before and was pleasantly surprised. The two of them ate and talked for an hour and Ronnie insisted on washing the dishes. As the weather was dry and fine, they walked to the shop to open up, still chatting and feeling more comfortable with each other with every passing minute. Elsie decided she was going to enjoy introducing this girl to some of the finer things in life when she returned from Milan.

*

The coat came back from the dry cleaner smelling as sweet as it did before being packed away. Elsie decided not to wear it until she left for Italy. It seemed an appropriate debut for something with an Italian named designer. So it was hung, free of any covering, in Elsie's wardrobe where she could see it every time she opened the door, which was at least twice a day. She tried not to gloat but just could not help the frisson of triumph which rippled through her every time.

It was cold and frosty on the morning of Elsie's departure to Milan. She had never learned to drive and, after

David died, used the same local taxi company whenever needed. She asked them to pick her up at the shop rather than home because she wanted to see Ronnie before leaving. As she was away for only four days, she packed her small case with the little wheels and handle to pull it along by. It stood in the hall by the full-length mirror. Elsie checked her handbag for essential contents, then picked up her coat.

Although she had tried it on several times since it returned to her, the feeling was nothing compared to putting the coat on to actually go out in and be seen. As she caressed the big velvet collar held close to her face and studied the effect in the mirror, she felt a rush of almost sensual joy. Elsie stepped outside, locked the door carefully and pulling her luggage along by the handle, proceeded on her walk of pride.

Several people smiled at her, calling out 'Good morning' and Elsie knew what it was like to be important, as the true reason for asking the car driver to come to the shop bore fruit. Ronnie had her back to the door when she heard its genteel chime. For a split second, she didn't recognise the figure in green with a bag on wheels.

"My goodness, Elly, it's you! You look wonderful," she said in genuine admiration.

"Thank you, dear. Glad you like it because I value the opinion of my new partner," replied a delighted Elsie. "That's why I've asked the car to pick me up here. And I've got something for you."

"You've given me so much already, I can't think what it could be that you've missed out," said Ronnie.

"It's a spare set of keys for the flat," said Elsie, fishing them out of her handbag. As my niece, I think you should have them because you never know. I've put you on my passport as a contact as well."

"Thank you so much. I won't take advantage, I promise," said Ronnie.

"I know, dear, I know," said Elsie, putting her arms round the girl affectionately, suddenly realising that she could indeed trust her with anything.

The door pinged again and there was the neatly suited taxi driver with a 'Mercury Cars' badge on his lapel. He took Elsie's bag, stowed it in the boot and held the door open for her. Ronnie stood waving at the kerb until the car was out of sight. Her growing fondness for her benefactor was genuine and she knew that, even in the midst of her new responsibilities, she would miss her.

The hire car was extremely comfortable, luxurious in fact. As they bowled smoothly along through the countryside, Elsie felt completely relaxed and happy. She also began to feel rather warm. As much as she enjoyed being cuddled into her coat, she decided to half take it off. It would be easy to slip into it again when they got to the airport. She undid the horn button and slid both arms out, laying the sleeves on either side of her. That felt much better.

Elsie sat back and thought about the coming fashion show and ideas for an Italian theme in the shop. Her right hand crept out to stroke the green velvet cuff which lay by her side. Warm and comfortable, she nearly fell asleep. Presently, she became aware that they were in a built-up area, moving slowly and she thought they must be getting near the airport. She looked out of the window and saw a bus ahead of them on the inside lane. When the queue of vehicles came to a standstill, Elsie noticed a young man dressed in a black parka with a knapsack on his back running along. As he passed her car he glanced in and she saw he was little more than a boy. He ran on to jump on the bus before everything began to move again. Elsie felt glad he had caught the bus. He had looked harassed and worried, as if he were late for school or something.

"We have plenty of time, Mrs Lehman. Don't worry," came the voice of the driver, speaking into his machine in the front. "We have reached some congestion in the traffic but we'll be free of it soon and at the airport in ten minutes."

Elsie resumed her pleasant reverie and they did indeed begin to move slowly. After a while, she saw that they had somehow changed lanes and were now alongside the bus. The last thing that Elsie saw was the terrified face of the boy who had been running, pressed against the bus window. Then there was a mighty roar and everything went red. Then black, then... nothing.

* * *

– 22 –

Reg Wilson drove what he affectionately called his leftovers wagon up to the barrier. He had his pass ready but didn't really need it. The policeman at the entrance knew him well and opened up quickly, letting Reg through then joining him when he came to a halt.

"Mornin', Joe. Nasty, very nasty," commented Reg, climbing down from the van and gazing around him.

"Nasty's not the word for this one. Eight dead on the bus including two kids, driver and passenger in the car. The others had various injuries. Both vehicles smashed to smithereens. Lucky it wasn't a bigger bomb, I suppose," said Joe.

"Who was it? Do they know yet?" asked Reg.

"Apparently two of the survivors saw a boy run for the bus and jump on in the traffic jam a way back. Dark, about twentyish and carrying a knapsack on his back," replied the police guard. "They reckoned it was him."

"Bloody terrorists," growled Reg. "Where's it all going to end, eh?"

"When the buggers have taken over the world, I suppose, or think they have. At the moment it's just small stuff here, not the same as New York or the London underground. A few unimportant people and kids dead, a main road to the airport closed off for more than twenty-four hours, mess all over the place, minor mayhem really," opined Joe glumly. "Doesn't stop me feeling sick, though, every time I see it's happened again."

"Me, too," agreed Reg, "and worrying about what sort of future my young 'uns are going to have. We're in the wrong job, mate. All we can do is clear up and hope it'll stop some day. Have the lab boys taken everything they want?"

"Yeah. It's all yours now, then the hoses can come in. We can open up the road again by teatime, hopefully. Be lucky, Reg."

Reg climbed back in his van and parked it by the barrier a bit further down on the other side of the road. He changed into his work coat and boots, got his broom, rubber gloves and a pile of plastic bags ready, then made a swift survey of the scene. They seemed to have done a thorough job of clearance already. There was less small rubbish scattered around than usual at these sites.

It was Reg's job to clear and tidy up the aftermath of bad road accidents. He moved in when all remains of vehicles and large objects had been removed, including things which might be needed as evidence, forensic tests and suchlike. It was a menial job but he was good at it and did it properly. The road would be opened again only when there was nothing left for the gawping public to gawp at, such as a tissue with a red splash on it, and Reg's job had been done.

He usually began in one corner and worked his way up and down in lines. That way, he didn't miss anything. When he had filled one plastic bag, he left it where it was and got a fresh one to start where he had left off. He was quite hardened to unpleasant looking stains on the ground. The hose crew would deal with those.

On the bus bomb site, Reg moved methodically to and fro, filling one bag fairly quickly. A couple of things gave him a small qualm. One was a crushed and filthy soft toy kangaroo and the other a little torn pink shoe. Reg thought of the two small children who had died and hoped that they had known nothing when it happened. Two bags later, nothing of more note than a comb with half its teeth missing, a squashed half-full cigarette box and a big blue marking pencil had made their appearance.

Reg got his broom, swept all the broken glass into piles and shovelled it into special strengthened bags. Bit by bit, it was all taken back to the leftovers wagon to be loaded. It was then that Reg noticed what appeared to be a blanket rumpled into the kerb by his rear wheel. He was sure it wasn't his and hadn't fallen out when he opened the back doors to load. He gave it a tweak and it opened out to reveal a strange looking hook or clasp of some kind. Another tweak convinced him that this was not a blanket. Even more vigorous tweaking and two unmistakable arms showed themselves. It was a coat, largely stained with dry blood.

Closer inspection of the sleeves revealed what looked like fur on the cuffs. Reg knew little about women's clothes and not much more about menswear save for his own sizes but he had a strange feeling about this wracked and spoiled garment. He found a smaller rubbish bag and bundled it in, tied up the top and put it in the front cab of the van. His job was finished now and he loaded all the rubbish bags into the back along with his tools. The hoses arrived and were waiting to take over. Reg drove off with a cheery wave to Joe and the others.

*

In a lay-by a couple of miles away, Reg pulled in to have a mug of tea from his thermos and a good think. He thought about his wife of twenty-four years, who he had loved dearly and deeply for all that time. She also loved him, gave him two healthy children, cooked cleaned and cared for him without complaint. Reg was not a clever or educated man but he was honest and hardworking. His job didn't pay all that well but it was the best he could do. There were small perks and he had two weeks' paid holiday every year. Usually, he spent some of that time doing jobs in the house and tiny garden.

Basically, Reg was a happy man. Yet he had one nagging regret and that was not earning enough to give Hilda, his wife, the good things he thought she deserved far more than most of the women he knew of. He gave her chocolates on her birthday and flowers sometimes but had always wished he had enough money to buy her good clothes and jewellery that she could show off. Some instinct told him that this coat he had found was special, if it wasn't damaged and could be made clean. It wouldn't be stealing because it was certainly rubbish to be incinerated. He had once found a broken bracelet on one of his clean-up sites and handed it in at the office. They had laughed at him and told him to get it mended and give it to his girlfriend. The jeweller he took it to said it wasn't gold but cheap Woolworths and not worth the cost of repairing. Not good enough for his Hilda by a long chalk so he had given it to the little girl next door to hang round her doll's neck.

Reg finished his tea and came to a decision. His brother-in-law, Bob, had a small but successful dry-cleaning business and they got on well together. He would take the coat to Bob when he had dumped all his rubbish and see what he thought.

*

As luck would have it, Bob was not busy. In fact, trade was usually a bit slack at midweek and he was glad of the distraction. He considered his brother-in-law a 'good egg' and thought his sister had done well to choose him above the other clever Dicks who fancied their chances at the time.

Once Reg had explained his dilemma, the two men laid a sheet on the floor in the back room, put some plastic gloves on and carefully straightened out the garment. Bob examined every inch, inside and out, in silence. Eventually, he sat back on his haunches and let out a long puff of breath through pursed lips.

"Well? What d'you think? Should I chuck it out?" asked Reg.

"My gawd, no. I wouldn't if I was you. Not this one," said Bob, standing up to ease his knees.

"I thought it might be special," Reg almost crowed, "Why, then?"

"Well, that's not cheap fur on the collar and cuffs, for a start. It's best velvet. Quality. The rest of it's pure wool with a satin lining. Then there's this single button, which is a kind of rare horn, not from a cow. There's not a bit of damage that I can see, not a stitch out of place, just a lot of caked-on blood. But this is the decider, look here," said Bob, bending down to fumble inside the coat. "A little label, here in the armpit. It says 'Anton Paloma'."

"Oh, yes. What's that then?" asked Reg.

"That, my friend, is a designer's name. Look, I've learned a lot in this business about clothes and a hidden name like that usually means it's a one-off. The only one of its kind. Everything about this coat shouts unique style and quality. I'd bet my all that somebody paid four figures for this originally."

"Good 'eavens," said Reg, his jaw dropping. "It must have belonged to the passenger from the back of the hire car, who was killed. It looks as if it would fit my Hilly a treat and she does love green. D'you reckon you could clean it up for me?"

"Course I can. Anything for you and my lovely sister. Just give me three or four days," said Bob.

"But say nothing, I haven't seen you. I haven't been here, right? You know what it is next week, don't you? Twenty-five years, eh!"

"Yeah. Mum's the word," replied Bob and the two men shook hands.

Reg went home on cloud nine. At last he would be able to give his Hilda something wonderful that nobody else had. His plans soared with his heart as he opened the front door. He was due some time off in place of overtime. They could go to Brighton for the weekend. She loved it there and she would look terrific in her new coat.

"I'm home, me darlin'. Pop the kettle on," he called out, his voice full of joy.

*

Exactly four days later, Bob was in the back room of his shop regarding his handiwork with pride. The coat was hanging on a rail in solitary splendour and it looked magnificent. All traces of stain had disappeared. The velvet collar and cuffs were softly smooth and seemed to glisten like glass as the light touched them. The beautiful horn button showed up palely in its green nest. Bob stroked the collar, feeling deep satisfaction with a job well done.

"You are a beaut, a real beaut," he told the coat. "Soon you are going to make someone so happy and proud."

He turned away and went to telephone his brother-in-law on his mobile with the good news.

* * *

– 23 –

News column from *The Daily Clarion*, Monday 28th February:

More and more reports have been coming in about gales and storms, especially in the South East. In Brighton yesterday, a woman was picked up bodily by a freak gust which hit the pier. Mrs Wilson was running for cover with her husband and several other people when the gale struck. She was borne along for ten yards and then was flung out to sea.

'It was weird,' a witness said. 'The wind seemed to get into her coat like a sail. It looked as if a huge green bird spread its wings and just flew away over the sea.'

The coastguard and lifeboat began an immediate search but so far there is no trace of Mrs Wilson. Her husband is said to be distraught and refuses to leave the seafront. The search resumed at first light this morning but hope of finding her alive is fading.

Mr and Mrs Wilson were on a second honeymoon trip. It was their 25th wedding anniversary.

* * *